Fight or Die

RICHARD FOREMAN

Sword of Rome Gladiator © Richard Foreman 2013.
A Brief Affair © Richard Foreman 2019.
A Knight's Tale © Richard Foreman 2020.
Raffles: The Gentleman Thief © Richard Foreman 2012.
"It's Everybody's Fight." © Richard Foreman 2013.

Richard Foreman has asserted his rights under the Copyright, Design and Patents Act, 1988, to be identified as the author of this work.

First published as a collection in 2021 by Sharpe Books.

CONTENTS

Introduction.
Sword of Rome: Gladiator
A Brief Affair
A Knight's Tale
Raffles: The Gentleman Thief
"It's Everybody's Fight"

FIGHT OR DIE

Introduction.

This book partly came into the world due to coincidence. During the course of a single week, I received three emails. The first two came from readers. One mentioned how much some of my shorter works had helped distract him during lockdown. The second reported how a couple of short stories I had contributed to the HWA collections of *Rubicon* and *By the Sword* had served as "a taster menu" to introduce him to the novels they were linked to. The third email was from the editor of Aspects of History, asking if I would like to contribute something to a forthcoming issue. These messages naturally got me thinking.

I must confess that cynicism, as well as coincidence, also prompted me to put this collection together. I have been able to re-heat and re-package some old dishes. There is an element of curation to this anthology, however. The title is *Fight or Die*. The protagonists, in some fashion, each decide to make a stand, whether fighting for themselves or a greater cause. I thought the theme was apt, given the year we have just endured. But the theme is secondary and not to be taken too seriously. Life is to be enjoyed as well as endured. Historical fiction should entertain more than educate. The stories contained in this collection were great fun to write. They are intended to be great fun to read too.

I was all too pleased to take a walk down memory lane and re-visit some of my previous works. What with being in lockdown, it was second best to being able to walk down to the pub. I am understandably fond of the characters and series that these short works relate to. I remember receiving plenty of emails from UK and US soldiers when the *Sword of Rome* series was published, saying how much they enjoyed the books when posted overseas. Who would have thought that soldiers enjoyed stories about war, drinking and whoring? *Raffles: A Gentleman Thief* allowed me to tick off writing about Sherlock Holmes from the bucket list. *A Brief Affair* gifted me the opportunity to re-visit one of my favourite heroes, or anti-heroes, in the form of Rufus Varro. I still receive comments about how much readers laugh at, or are offended by, the opening paragraphs of *Spies of Rome: Blood & Honour*. *A Knight's Tale* afforded me the opportunity to fix a dropped stitch in the *Crusaders* series, by including a Varangian or two in the story. "It's Everybody's Fight" can be found in *The Complete Pat Hobby*. Although the book is far from being my bestselling project, it may be the funniest and most underrated work.

I duly hope that you appreciate the following taster menu, and it provides some food for thought – and gives you an appetite to read other titles in the various series. Feel free to get in touch if you do. You never know, your email may prompt me to write another book.

Richard Foreman.
London. 2021.

Sword of Rome: Gladiator

1.

"She kept me up all night, even when I was dreaming of her in my sleep," Roscius expressed, still smirking fondly, remembering the previous evening's drinking and whoring. The hung-over soldier then reached for a nearby jug of water and gulped down its contents in an effort to rehydrate himself.

"Was she clean?" his centurion asked. Lucius Oppius did not mind his men enjoying themselves, but he did not want them catching a pox either. He had let his unit sleep in, but he finally roused them. He wanted to reach the city by the close of day. They had both time and money to spend in Rome over the coming days – a reward from Caesar for having completed a special mission for their general during the battle of Alesia. Oppius brushed his hand in front of his face, but it did little to diminish the thick odour of sweat and wine which hung in the air of the room at the inn.

"No, fortunately she was filthy," the hulking infantryman replied, giggling like a schoolboy at his own joke. "She was uncommonly attractive, for a whore. Thankfully she was common in all sorts of other ways though. But still my piece couldn't compare to the girl we picked out for Fabius, eh lad?"

The young, studious legionary, who owned aspirations of becoming a poet, blushed and grinned sheepishly in the corner. His blushes could still not disguise his red-rimmed eyes however.

"Her breasts were an eyeful, handful and no doubt mouthful," Teucer, a skilled archer from Britain who Caesar had recruited to the Tenth Legion, exclaimed whilst simultaneously yawning.

Fabius rolled his eyes, as he considered how he was planning to introduce the unit to his mother over a supper at his family home just outside of Rome.

"The lad has probably already run out of ink, writing poems to her," Roscius remarked.

"He certainly must have run out of something for her. He didn't get back until only a few hours ago," Teucer added, winking at the youth.

"She's doubtless taken his heart," Roscius said, following up his jug of water with a swig of sour wine.

"More likely she's taken the contents of his purse. There's always fresh meat to fuel the oldest profession," Teucer posited.

"Aye, and the one you picked last night was so old she could have been one of the founders of the trade."

"I would try and defend her honour and virtue but I fear she lost those during the reign of Sulla," the Briton joked.

Despite having warned his men not to have too raucous a night the officer would refrain from saying anything to Fabius, partly because he was also guilty of staying out late. Oppius had spent the evening with one of the servant girls at the inn, Florentia. He had not long left her side. Oppius had promised the pretty, blonde girl that he would see her again on his way back. Florentia had promised that she would stay faithful to him until that time. Both would break their promises, though neither would be broken-hearted as a result. Nevertheless the lissom, fun wench had proved a welcome distraction. For once he had not spent half the night awake, thinking about Livia - a former agent of Caesar's and Oppius' ex-lover. She had betrayed him in Gaul, yet had spared his life. Memories and images of the seductive woman often still jabbed through the ribcage of his thoughts.

"Was she worth it?" the centurion remarked, turning to the youth.

The once sweet-faced Fabius nodded in reply, whilst this time wolfishly grinning.

Oppius had frequently asked himself the same question in regards to Livia. The answer was not always the same. He knew not if he would kiss her – or kill her - should he ever see her again.

2.

Oppius gave a few coins to a farmer heading towards the city so that the four soldiers travelled in the back of a wagon on the final leg of their journey. Rome never ceased to take a man's breath away, or give him a crick in the neck, as he craned his head upwards to take in the famed seven hills – from the Subura to the Palatine, with its gleaming white villas. Clouds scudded across the sky above but they could still not shut out the will of the gods to have the sun bathe the Olympus-like city in light. Streaks of smoke poured upwards from Rome's various bakeries and forges. The murmur of thousands of voices could be heard from outside the walls; the voices were separate, yet also bound together in an inexplicable chorus – or sometimes dirge - of sound. Traffic streamed in and out of the city gates, kicking up dust. The city swallowed up an endless procession of mules and wagons laden with olives, grapes, barley, salted pork and other assorted produce. A white bull slowly – and seemingly sadly – entered the city, perhaps foreseeing its role in an imminent pagan sacrifice. Immigrants of all colours and creeds, dressed in rags and carrying all their worldly goods in small bundles, gaped in fear and wonder at their new home. Rome and the surrounding view, as the soldiers made their way along the Via Salaria, was also home to various gardens, fields, theatres, monuments and snaking aqueducts. The roads were lined with tombs, from the austere to the elaborate. Fabius mused to himself how all roads led to Rome, but really all roads lead to one's grave. He made a note of the concept, in order to include it in a future poem.

Oppius thought how Rome was a monster; it fed itself on a diet of martial glory, dramatic spectacles, political demagogues and religious fervour. Rome had also seemingly thirsted for blood over the centuries too. The walls had run red with Tarquin the Proud, the Gracchi, the supporters of Sulla and Marius - and Catiline and his conspirators. The walls were currently painted with graffiti about Caesar and Pompey – but would the paint be ultimately washed away in the blood of a civil war between the great men?

Before Rome imploded again though, Oppius would enjoy the city. He who is tired of Rome is tired of life, he had heard Fabius once say, quoting another poet. The centurion looked forward to visiting a bath house and feeling the water, strigil and massage oils upon his skin, soothing body and mind. He would doubtless also accompany his unit when they ventured down to the bars and brothels in the Subura one evening; the Subura was the place where everyone liked to visit but no one liked to live. He would decline an invite to any gladiatorial bout however. Although Oppius could understand the popularity of the spectacle and the crowd baying for blood that did not mean that he appreciated the "sport". The centurion had witnessed enough death and cruelty through his job. He could do without their spectres when free from his duties.

As the wagon passed through the Collina gate Teucer gently whistled through his teeth in awe at the scale and otherworldliness of the city, albeit he was less enamoured with the pungent smell of horse dung assaulting his nostrils.

"Not even you could drink this town dry Roscius," the Briton exclaimed, thinking how London had a long way to go to match the wonder and enormity of Rome.

"No, but I'm going to have fun trying," the legionary replied, licking his lips in anticipation of the days ahead. "I'll begin by working my way through Fabius' family cellar during dinner this evening. Most of the vintages are even older that the whore you slept with last night."

"But will they taste as sweet?" the Briton replied with a lewd grin and wink.

"Yes. Because the wine will be free."

"You'll pay for the wine if you drink too much though. We've still got some business to attend to tomorrow morning, delivering some correspondence for Caesar. Roscius, you and I will be venturing over to the Aventine Hill to deliver a letter to a merchant, Sextus Mallius. Fabius, I want you to deliver a letter to Caesar's great nephew, Octavius. Teucer, you can accompany him."

"Do you not want to visit the young Caesar yourself? He could prove to be a powerful patron in years to come," Fabius asserted.

"Having one Caesar as a patron is proving dangerous enough. If the young Caesar starts ordering me around too, it could prove the death of me," the centurion humourlessly joked.

3.

Titus Fabius still had the same distinctive scarred, shaven head from when he had been a soldier, but the former officer's once flint-like features had softened with age and good living. His waistline had grown as had his income since retiring from his twenty-five years of service in the army. Titus was now a wealthy merchant, having invested in a number of mining projects in Greece. He lived in one of the largest properties on the Quirinal Hill, having bought the villa because the bedroom overlooked the Campus Martius. "It's nice to be reminded about where you've come from," Titus remarked to Oppius, who had once served as a raw recruit under the veteran centurion.

"The pornography's mine. All the serious books are his," Titus exclaimed, smiling and nodding towards his son. Fabius rolled his eyes and looked embarrassed - akin to any youth in the presence of a half-drunk father. Oppius and his unit were being given a tour of Titus' house. They were in the library, where the merchant's slaves commenced to serve his guests with wine and various dishes of finger foods (olives, mixed nuts, dates, figs, plums, mussels and snails).

"I must thank you again Lucius for taking care of Marcus. He left here a boy, but he has returned a man. He was as wet as a sardine when he first joined the legion, but there's now more of a hardness to him," Titus said, looking fondly at his eldest son and admiring his new soldierly physique.

Roscius was here about to add that there was certainly a hardness to Marcus the night before in the brothel, but thankfully his mouth was more concerned with making the most of the food than making a joke.

"He's taken as much care of me as I have of him, I dare say," Oppius replied, modestly.

"It does seems you need looking after sometimes my old friend. I read about your act of bravery, or rather lunacy, on the shores of Britain, when you helped take the beach. The despatches about the engagement had men cheering and raising their glasses to the standard bearer of the Tenth. Women probably swooned too. When I asked you to take care of Marcus I thought it was implied that you should take care of yourself too."

"It wasn't reported in the despatches, but Marcus saved my life during the invasion – I'm glad to say. I'm not sure how glad he was about it though, after all the drilling and dangerous situations I've put him through since. But Marcus has turned into a fine young man and soldier, Titus."

"I believe you. I do not provide him with a generous enough allowance to bribe you into saying complimentary things. But I warrant that I do not just have you to thank for keeping an eye out for the lad. I suspect that you too have also had a hand in his protection and education," Titus remarked, turning towards Roscius and Teucer.

"Aye, I guess I taught the lad how to hold a bow and shoot straight," the archer wryly conceded.

"And I taught him how to hold his drink and not shoot his mouth off," Roscius added, grinning with visible pleasure and pride at the witticism he had just come up with.

"You have my thanks," Titus warmly exclaimed, clasping his hands upon the two men's shoulders. "My door will always be open to you. But right now let me open up my kitchen and wine cellar to you both."

Just as Teucer had once believed that the attacks upon the Roman defences at Alesia would never end, so too he wondered if the procession of slaves bringing out different dishes of food would carry on throughout the night. Various foodstuffs on silver plates covered all three tables in the opulent dining room:

leeks in mushroom sauce, spiced pork, salted tuna upon a bed of lettuce, stuffed eels, lamprey, wild fowl, radishes in garum, partridge in garum, asparagus in garum, sardines in garum, wood pigeon, various cheeses and more. Even though their host was discussing the fate and future of Rome, the archer could not help but be transfixed by the aromatic feast before him.

"It's a matter of simple arithmetic. There can only be one First Man of Rome. This city will not be big enough for the both of them. Caesar and Pompey will clash, as sure as the seas crash against the shores. Pompey will not permit any equal, Caesar will not admit any superior. Any hope of a peace between them died with Julia I warrant – Caesar's daughter and Pompey's wife. For Rome, it was a match made in heaven. Pompey has yet to officially break with Caesar, but I know that Cato has been whispering poison into his ears, as well as openly denigrating Caesar in the Forum."

"Who do you believe will be the last man standing?" Marcus asked his father, losing his appetite at the thought of a conflict which could tear the world in two. He blanched, imagining that the bloody battles and scorched plains of Gaul could spread to the Italian peninsular and pit Roman against Roman.

"Caesar has spent the last ten years sharpening the swords of his legions, whilst Pompey has exited the theatre of war. His military prowess may now be akin to an old, unused blade – which has spent too long housed in its scabbard. Yet Pompey currently holds the ground, Rome itself. As you know military thinking dictates that an attacker normally needs three times the force of the defender to take a fortified town. Yet Caesar may only raise a third of the forces that Pompey could have at his disposal. So again it could just come down to a matter of arithmetic. But Caesar has defied the odds before. Cicero once made a speech about how Pompey possessed the key virtues of a great general, namely courage, military knowledge, authority and good luck. Caesar not only possesses a surplus of the first three of those virtues but I warrant that he could even turn Pompey's good luck into better luck. However, the storm brewing between Caesar and Pompey is on the distant horizon. I would have you look to the clouds that could be hanging over yourselves right now."

"What do you mean?" Oppius asked, topping up his men's wine with water.

"Caesar is not the only person to employ agents to keep him informed and watch his enemies. Cato and Pompey doubtless are aware of your presence in Rome – and your task to deliver some of Caesar's correspondence. Watch your backs lads. The backstreets of Rome may prove more dangerous than the battlefields of Gaul. At least you faced your enemy there and knew what was coming. My advice to you is to keep your heads down and lay low."

A short pause here ensued while the four comrades looked at each other, unsure of how much they should trust in their host's warnings and advice. Even Roscius paused in necking his wine. Yet after draining his cup he spoke:

"I intend to spend many an hour lying low – below the female population of the Subura. It'll be fine. We're off duty. I'm no more an agent of Caesar's than I am a fishmonger."

Although off duty Oppius still ordered his unit to sharpen their blades that evening, before they went to bed.

4.

Morning.

A watery light seeped into the narrow streets as Teucer and Marcus Fabius made their way across the city to deliver Caesar's correspondence to his great-nephew. The Briton could not help but be amused and captivated by the sights, sounds and – less so – smells of Rome. He swung his head left and right to take in the colourful and novel scenes of Rome waking up, yet at the same time he needed to keep an eye on the ground as the archer dodged left and right to avoid stepping into the excrement beneath his feet.

"This city is full of history – but it is also full of shit," Fabius remarked, quoting a line from one of his own poems.

The streets soon grew wider – and cleaner – however, as they made their way towards the Palatine district and their destination.

The slave who opened the door to the legionaries seemed to have had his nose broken more times than Teucer had broken his bowstring. Grunts supplanted speech as the attendant – a former gladiator who now served as one of many bodyguards to the young Caesar – led the soldiers through the large house out into the garden, where they found Octavius sitting beneath a cypress tree, reading.

The boy immediately removed his sun hat and got up to greet the messengers as soon as he saw them. He wore a white tunic with a subtle purple border. His hair was fair, his complexion pale – to the point of appearing sickly. Yet his blue eyes shone with friendliness and intelligence. His build was slight and Fabius thought to himself how Caesar's great-nephew had spent more time in the library than on the Campus Martius.

Fabius, who had spent a similar amount of time exercising his mind – rather than body – as a young teenager, looked over to see what Octavius had been reading, after handing over the letters and exchanging pleasantries and news about his great-uncle and the campaign in Gaul. The would-be poet raised his eyebrow in pleasant surprise to discover that the youth was reading Catullus.

"Now he is treading that dark road to the place from which they say no one has ever returned."

Despite the weak light Roscius still squinted as he gazed up at the sky, accompanying Oppius to hand Caesar's letters over to Sextus Mallius at his house on the Aventine Hill of Rome. In answer to the accusation of being hung-over the legionary replied that he was just "tired". The property was extensive – and expensive. Crassus had once owned the house. Suffice to say the build quality of the residence was superior to those houses that the former triumvir had constructed for his numerous tenants. Mallius had been described – and labelled in graffiti – as being a "new Crassus". The first man to call him such had been Cicero (the satirical statesman having given him the nickname in order to denigrate the affluent and influential merchant). But Mallius took pride in the title and thought it a compliment. Mallius even took to adopting some of Crassus' business practices, as well as his maxims, as a result. "Loyalty and friends can be bought, rather than earned." Although the merchant and banker often trumpeted that he was a self-made man in terms of his income (he owned property and mining interests, as well as a string of gladiator schools) most of his wealth stemmed from a fortuitous inheritance.

Oppius and Roscius were led into a half-lit triclinium. When someone once asked Mallius why he kept his house so gloomy he replied that "darkness is cheaper than light". Yet still the light was good enough for the merchant to look at – and look down upon – the soldiers cum messengers. His eyes were two slits – full of idle, or active, disdain for the world. His face also housed a downturned mouth and aquiline nose. His skin was leathery, his build was lean. Titus had given his opinion of Mallius at dinner the previous night, yet the centurion would have come to the same conclusion about the merchant on his own accord soon enough. Mallius viewed Rome as not something that he should serve, but something that he could exploit. He lay upon his couch as if it were a throne.

"Well don't just stand there you fools! Which one of you slabs of meat possesses these letters from Caesar?" There was a slight sibilance and shrillness to the merchant's voice. Roscius would comment after the meeting that Mallius owned both a "woman's voice and girl's figure".

Oppius walked over to Mallius and handed over the correspondence. The merchant neither thanked nor looked at the soldier as he did so – but merely thrust out his arm and grabbed the packet.

"Now wait here whilst I go through them, in case I need to give a reply immediately," the sour-faced financier remarked. Mallius proceeded to read Caesar's letters upon the large sofa, often adjusting his toga whilst he read, as the garment failed to cling comfortably to his slight figure. He neither offered his guests refreshments nor permitted them to sit down.

The centurion was already aware of the nub of Caesar's message, as his commander had confided in him. Mallius was in possession of certain pieces of intelligence in regards to which senators were for or against him retaining his legions, should he return to Rome. The aged merchant's eyes both widened and narrowed whilst he read the letters. He hummed and grunted a couple of times but by the end he seemed content – to the point of licking his lips in satisfaction or expectation.

"You are Oppius?" Mallius remarked; this time fixing his eyes upon the centurion intently, as a critic may appraise a new piece of sculpture.

"Yes."

"Now you are - mine," the wily looking merchant replied after a pause, his downturned mouth transforming itself into a serpentine grin.

5.

"My mind's sunk so low, Claudia, because of you, wrecked itself on your account so bad already, that I couldn't like you if you were the best of women, - or stop loving you, no matter what you do," Fabius exclaimed, quoting his favourite lines from Catullus. He briefly paused as he thought of Oppius and Livia in relation to the extract, before adding that,

"Unrequited love is perhaps the only true love."

"Then give me plenty of a love that's false," Teucer replied, in between mouthfuls of his honey-glazed pork.

The young Octavius smiled, enjoying both the idealism of Fabius and the cynicism of his comrade. Octavius had asked the soldiers to stay for an early lunch and questioned them more in regards to Caesar and the Gallic campaign.

"You have an accent. May I ask where you're originally from?"

"Britain. You can take the boy out of Britain, but you can't completely take Britain out of the boy," the archer answered.

"And how would you describe your countrymen?"

"They are mad when they're drunk – and mad when they're sober," Teucer concluded, after a brief moment's thought.

"I do not mean to give offence to your homeland but I have heard that Britain is still largely a barbarous land, especially in the north. It is in need of laws – and bread and circuses. Once we start providing these then we might be able to civilise the people, wean them off their drink."

"Stop the British from drinking? Now who's mad?" Teucer remarked, amused at the proposition.

"I am but mad north-north-west," Octavius wryly replied, quoting a line from a play which was familiar to Fabius also. "Let me thank you again for having come so far, from the north-west, to deliver these letters though. I hope I will see you both once more before you return. I may have letters for you to give to Caesar if so."

"You may wish to give them to Lucius Oppius, our centurion. He has Caesar's ear and can deliver any messages personally," Fabius said, increasingly impressed by the boy's intelligence, politeness and wit. He was mature beyond his years – possessing genuine virtues as opposed to just being precocious.

"My great-uncle has mentioned him in his correspondence. He called him one of the bravest soldiers in his army."

Teucer thought to himself how Oppius was as bloody-minded as he was bloody brave. He was intrigued as to how the studious youth and tough centurion would get on however, should they ever meet.

Oppius' face began to screw itself up as much as his fist as he read over the letters. The first was addressed to Mallius and mentioned how Caesar was willing to lend him the use of his centurion, as well pay him handsomely, for the information he wanted. The second letter, contained in the packet, was addressed to Oppius himself. Caesar first apologised for the position he was putting his centurion in, but the intelligence the merchant possessed was extremely valuable to him. Caesar also stated how he would financially compensate Oppius and his unit should Mallius make use of his offer during the soldier's stay in Rome. Oppius cursed his commander beneath his breath as he read his orders – and Mallius spoke whilst he took in the letter again.

"I am a merchant and one of the commodities I trade in is knowledge. As you are discovering I have a piece of knowledge to sell – and I have a buyer. Caesar has offered me a sum of gold, as well as your services and labour, as payment for this knowledge. I'm willing to accept the terms. As you may already be aware I own a number of gladiator schools. I also arrange gladiatorial contests for the populace in various arenas in and around the city. The mob's manners may be bad, but its money is good. I have arranged an event for the day after tomorrow in a sizeable arena just outside Ostia, but I am one combatant short due to injury. I could of course call upon a piece of meat from one of my own schools, but it strikes me that you might add a certain glamour to the bill. You are the famous standard bearer who led the charge during the invasion of Britain. You have just come back victorious from the siege of Alesia. Yes, you will provide something extra I believe. You are an accomplished soldier. Let us hope that you prove an equally competent gladiator, for your sake more than mine," Mallius issued, and then let out a nasty little laugh.

As much as he felt he owed Mallius nothing (or less than nothing, such was his growing dislike for the odious merchant) Oppius still owed a duty to Caesar. Caesar had promoted him and taken the centurion into his trust. He had rewarded him well for his service – and felt his commander would display a similar loyalty to him should somehow their roles be reversed.

"You can of course refuse, but nobody will win if that proves the case. Caesar will not receive his intelligence and I will not get paid. You may also find yourself earning your commander's displeasure. Not an enviable fate I suspect. If you have any doubts, I can assure you that your opponent will not be of the highest standard."

The effete merchant took a visible pleasure in wielding a certain amount of power over the centurion. He thought to himself how yet again brains were conquering brawn. Rome was Rome because of the patrician and merchant classes. The mob merely existed to raise their superiors up even higher. Even the success of the Roman army was due to the few leading the many – lions leading donkeys – Mallius concluded.

"So, centurion, do we have an accord?"

"Put together the names on a list for Caesar – and you can put my name down on the bill for the contest," Oppius answered, looking as though the next person that he would kill would be the merchant, as opposed to any rival in an arena.

6.

Oil glistened all over the gladiator's muscular body. He snorted and grinned, revealing a set of yellow teeth pillaged from the mouths of his various victims in the arena. Although "Aulus the Mauler" was not of the highest standard of combatants, as Mallius had promised, he was still of a "high" standard, Titus Fabius had assured Oppius. The centurion stood next to his fearsome opponent in the tunnel. As an extra piece of theatre, or authenticity, Mallius suggested that the soldier wear his uniform when fighting the veteran gladiator. Oppius carried his gladius and scutum. Mallius had also ordered one of his attendants to clean-up the centurion's breastplate and greaves.

Aulus tensed up next to his opponent, flexing his muscles in order to intimidate the slightly smaller soldier. The gladiator's body was a lattice-work of scars. His long, lank hair could still not hide his large cauliflower ears. Aulus turned towards Oppius and gifted him a hostile, unblinking look whilst flaring his nostrils. Titus warned his friend how the gladiator would attempt to intimidate him beforehand, "There's many an opponent that he's defeated even before they have stepped out onto the sand... Aulus is quicker than his bulk suggests. He also knows as many dirty moves as a legionary. Even more perhaps. Yet his weaknesses will be his over-confidence and his need to play to the crowd. A few more like Aulus however and Spartacus might now be residing in a villa on top of the Palatine. He's a brutal bastard that even his mother would have trouble loving."

Oppius merely rolled his eyes in reply to the gladiator's attempt to overawe him.

"You all set?" Roscius asked, warmly clasping his friend on the shoulder.

"Aye. Are we all set? Did you get a good price?" the centurion replied, making reference to the bets that Oppius had asked his legionary to place on his behalf.

"I got a great price. You're far from the favourite."

"I'm unsure as to whether that's good news or not."

"The prize may not just be your winnings. I've heard that the wife of a senator will invite the victor back to her villa. Apparently she likes gladiators, or soldiers," Roscius said, raising his eyebrow suggestively.

"Some trophies are not worth keeping. I've seen her. She's even too old for Teucer. If she likes soldiers tell her I'm a gladiator. If she likes gladiators tell her I'm a soldier."

Roscius wished his friend good luck and then disappeared to join his comrades at their seats in the arena.

"I'm gonna make you wish you never left Gaul and your legion," Aulus remarked in a rasping voice, sneering at his opponent.

"I wish that already."

"I'm gonna teach you the meaning of the word pain."

"You sound like my ex-wife. If your tactic is to bore me to death then you're succeeding."

Aulus snarled, but before he could utter anything else the gladiators were instructed to follow the umpire and arena slaves out onto the sand.

The roar from the crowd assaulted his ears to the point that Oppius even flinched a little. A thousand cheers and jeers were spat forth. Some called out Aulus' name, either in denigration or celebration. The centurion briefly took in some of the enraptured spectators. Many were wide-eyed, lusting for violence. Wine-stained teeth were also bared, in smiles or hisses. Women shrieked. Oppius became slightly disorientated as hundreds of people he neither knew – nor desired to know - called out his name. He squinted in the light of the sun and placed his hand in front of his face. Many were dressed in their brightest and best clothes; perhaps the men folk had told their wives that they were visiting the temple. The audience undulated as it rose and sat down together.

Aulus acknowledged the crowd, which only fuelled the frenzy. The retiarius (or "net man") jabbed his spear up in the air and also swung his net, fishing for their attention and adulation. A cold sun hung in a pale blue sky. His muscles rippled, the oil upon his skin gleamed as if he was made of polished bronze. Oppius observed his opponent, scrutinising his body for any past injuries he could exploit. The centurion had spent the previous day training with Titus and Roscius, working through the offensive and defensive capabilities of the retiarius. One had to get past the point of the spear, whilst also avoiding the danger of being trapped or tripped by the net. Titus drilled him hard; by dusk Oppius began to win as many practise bouts as he lost.

"Hear that centurion? That applause is for me. You may be a big noise in the theatre of war, but this is my stage – and I'm the lead actor on it. I intend to put on a show."

Again the gladiator raised his arms up triumphantly, as though the bout was over and he was already victorious. Oppius watched the arena slaves scatter extra sand on the ground, to soak up the puddles of blood – as Aulus continued to soak up the atmosphere. "The Battle of the Beasts," a contest between a drugged up rhinoceros and elephant, had preceded the gladiatorial combat. From the amount of blood and gore Oppius could discern beneath the sand it appeared that both had perished in the fight.

A trumpet sounded and the arena's umpire made a brief announcement. Oppius drew his sword. The centurion had taken down bigger, stronger and quicker – but not like this.

The umpire ordered the combat to commence.

Aulus the Mauler took his customary wide stance. He then spread his arms, turned his head up to the sky and gave out a mighty roar. It was the last line the colourful gladiator would ever deliver upon his stage. Noticing his bare torso as a wide open target and his eyes averted towards the sky Oppius grasped his chance. The sharpened gladius cut through the air – and cut into his chest and lungs, choking out the net man's battle cry.

A stunned silence was swiftly succeeded by an explosion of cheers and boos, even greater to that of before the bout. Some spectators felt cheated out of a proper fight, yet others marvelled at the soldier's audacity and skill. In the stands Roscius offered up a silent prayer of thanks to Mars and Fortuna. Teucer meanwhile clapped his hands, before dashing off to collect the unit's winnings.

The boos soon started to outnumber the cheers as Oppius ignored the audience's clamour for him to acknowledge them, or his triumph. Didn't someone tell him that he was here for their entertainment? Coriolanus was less contemptuous of the people, a senator who was in the crowd commentated to his mistress. The soldier continued to ignore the abuse and praise from the crowd as he walked over to his slain opponent. The colour was already draining from his face. His tongue poked out from his crooked set of teeth.

"Show's over," Oppius remarked, as he removed his sword from the still twitching corpse.

7.

News of the centurion's victory – and the novel and dramatic manner of Aulus the Mauler's defeat – travelled back to Rome before even Oppius and his unit were back inside the city walls. The tavern in the Subura, where Roscius and Teucer spent most of their evening, was abuzz with reports (some accurate, some fictitious) about the day's events in the arena at Ostia. Some considered the soldier's victory unsporting and that the spectators should have demanded their money back. Others felt a sense of pride – and security – that the centurion had defeated a gladiator; it augured well if ever a new Spartacus rose up to take on the legions.

When Roscius and Teucer returned to Titus Fabius' villa, in time to soak up the wine with another feast their host had arranged for them, they recounted a list of nicknames that Oppius was now being called: "Soldier of Fortune", "Caesar's Champion", "Oppius the Aulus Mauler". Marcus Fabius added to the list, by reporting upon a fresh piece of graffiti he had seen.

"The cartoon labelled you as the "Sword of Rome". I'm not sure it'll catch on. The image had you with a sword between your legs. Unfortunately for you they drew a gladius, rather than spartha."

"You have made a name for yourself it seems," Roscius exclaimed, feasting his eyes at the new batch of dishes that were being placed before him (red mullet, goose liver, pumpkin, beans in garum, wild boar chops in garum, lobster claws in garum). The legionary also feasted his eyes upon the dish of the serving girl who was attending to him. Either she was afflicted with a facial tic, or the buxom slave was winking at him whilst she served the soldier.

"Making a name for yourself can be as much of a curse as a blessing in this city," Titus posited, Cassandra-like in his tone and expression.

"You worry too much father," Marcus replied, just about winning his fight to separate the meat from the bone upon his chop.

"It's wisdom, as well as worry, which has turned what little hair I have left grey lad. Caesar's enemies might look to attack Caesar's Champion, in the absence of Caesar himself. You may also have become a victim of your own success in the eyes of Sextus Mallius. He'll reason that your new found fame will be able to put bums on seats."

"We had a deal. One fight, in exchange for the list."

"Never trust a banker Lucius. He will change his mind as easily as he'll change his rates of interest. Given the current state of affairs, the safest place for you may well be in the arena," Titus stated, wishing that he could have been solely joking.

8.

"I've known whores, or politicians even, who are more honest," Oppius exclaimed as he came out of Sextus Mallius' villa, accompanied by Marcus Fabius. Their meeting with the merchant had been brief. Mallius had given the centurion half the list, but argued that as he had added to the intelligence over the past day he wanted to alter the contract so that Oppius would fight one more time for him in the arena. Such was the promoter's confidence in Oppius - that he would sell out the arena - the merchant was even willing to give the lowly soldier a cut of the profits – a gesture that was unheard of normally, Mallius added magnanimously.

"I can help furnish you with both riches and fame," he uttered, jangling as he did so from all the jewellery (amulets, bangles and rings) he was wearing.

"I don't want fame or riches. I just want to go home," Oppius replied with frustration, remembering how he had still to visit his mother. Home however was perhaps now the legion, he considered. Either way, home was not the politic and decadent city of Rome he realised.

"Your home isn't going anywhere, however you are! Half the city wants to see you in the arena – and the other half wants to see you dead! It's perfect. Caesar, more than anyone, would want you to fight again too. You are his champion!"

The merchant's eyes gleamed like two gold coins, envisioning the spectacle and gate receipts of the famous standard bearer fighting again.

"You have a talent for killing it seems. It would be a crime to let your gift go to waste," Mallius softly said, looking to flatter the soldier, as he also lasciviously eyed two young slave boys standing in the corner, ready to bathe and massage their master.

"My talents extend to killing outside the arena too – and I don't just specialise in killing gladiators," Oppius replied, menacingly. The centurion was tempted to slit the man-snake's throat there and then. Yet unlike the state sponsored murder of gladiatorial combat he would be put on trial for killing the financier in his home. As "Caesar's Champion" the Senate would also hunt him down and prosecute with extreme prejudice. Not even Cicero would be able to save him, should he serve as his advocate.

Mallius left him to think over the new proposal and to give his answer in the morning, but both men knew that Oppius would strap his sword on again and enter the arena. The centurion hoped the next bout would be as equally brief and undemanding as the first. Mallius assured the soldier that his opponent "would not be the best that Rome had to offer".

Rain spat down from a sky as grey as a wolf pelt. Oppius thanked Fabius for accompanying him but the centurion now dismissed the young legionary.

"Consider the rest of the day your own Fabius. You might like to compose an ode and elegy for me, in light of the forthcoming fight. That way you will be covered regardless of the outcome," Oppius grimly joked, but smiled not.

Once his legionary was out of sight the centurion sighed and his shoulders dropped. His first thought was that he needed a drink. Mallius was even running his ex-wife a close second for the person who had heaped most misery upon him inside the city walls. Oppius also felt a creeping resentment towards Caesar. A drink, or several drinks, would help take his mind off things. He also thought how he was a short walk away from one of his ex-lovers, Fabia. She had been the wife of a quaestor then. He was now probably a praetor – and as such would seldom be spending time at home. She always dressed to impress; her outfits would take an age to put on, yet a moment to take off.

He could still hear the rustle of her silk stola as they made love in her curtained litter. If time had not ravished her, he would. Yet more than any patrician's wife Oppius missed and desired Livia. But it was a desire infected with grief. She had to be dead to him now. Should he go and visit Fabia, to see if she was home? Or, as he had money in his pocket, he could just as well visit a whore to help take his mind off things. There was little difference between them. Indeed Fabia would want him to buy her a piece of jewellery as tribute (she called such pieces of jewellery from her lovers "trophies"), which would end up costing him more than an hour or two with any prostitute.

"You Lucius Oppius?" The voice was stern, rough and abrupt.

"Are you asking me a question, or telling me I'm him?" Oppius answered, sizing up the man who had accosted him.

"My name is Rufus Glaber. I am an attendant to Marcus Porcius Cato. You will accompany me to see him. This is an order rather than question."

Oppius noticed how he was surrounded by four other men, all wearing identical white tunics with a black border. All had the build of former soldiers or gladiators, yet such were their severe and drear expressions that Oppius fancied they could have been former lictors also. He surveyed Glaber in particular. He stood – attempting to be imposing – with his arms folded across his barrelled chest. His body was taut and athletic, his jaw firm and neck bull-like. His green eyes were cold, yet focused. Oppius recognised a fellow officer when he saw one. The centurion weighed up his chances of fighting, or fleeing.

"You're quick and you're good Oppius, but you're not that quick and that good," Glaber remarked, reading the centurion's thoughts. With a nod of his head the four men surrounding Oppius moved in a little closer. "You're a rat caught in a trap. It'll be pointless to run or struggle. We don't mean you any harm, yet."

"I hear Cato keeps a good wine cellar. I'll come willingly."

Glaber's men subtly walked either side of Oppius as they made their way over to Cato's residence.

"I served in the Ninth, should you be wondering. Thankfully I was given a way out of the army though. The pay is better this side of the fence. I still possess a vine stick to keep discipline. I am also free from latrine duties," the ever alert mercenary remarked, wishing to either put himself above the centurion or instil envy in him.

"It's my experience that everyone has to deal with some sort of shit every day, no matter what they do."

"You're right. Today I have to deal with you," Glaber replied, with thinly veiled contempt.

"If ever you have to deal with me in earnest, you might wish you were back on latrine duty." Steel glinted in his eye. Oppius had encountered many an officer like Glaber before. Those that had tried to break a vine stick over his back had ended up with a broken nose. Respect needed to be earned through more than just possessing a bull-neck and superior attitude. Perhaps Mallius could arrange things for Cato's "attendant" to enter the arena too.

"Caesar's Champion also possesses Caesar's arrogance it seems."

"What might prove unfortunate for you is that Caesar's Champion is lacking in Caesar's clemency." The steel grew even harder, and sharper, in the centurion's gaze as he wryly smiled at the scowling mercenary.

9.

His grey eyes were red-rimmed from drinking, as Oppius recalled Titus' comment the night before:

"If Cato does speak the truth then it is wine-truth, such are the amounts he imbibes. He is temperate in everything, aside from his intemperance."

Although it was mid-afternoon the shutters to the austere triclinium were still half closed. Cato squinted in the half light however, as though suffering from a headache. The famous senator had a ruddy complexion, unkempt hair and wore an unwashed toga. Glaber warned Oppius that his master might seem tired, as he had spent the evening debating philosophy and politics with a number of other patricians and philosophers. Most that had attended would have said they spent the evening drinking. The senator put down his book, rose up from his cedar wood chair and took in his guest. "He looked like he was chewing a wasp," Oppius would tell Titus later that evening, in regards to describing the aristocrat's expression when addressing the soldier. "If it's any consolation Cato looks down on everyone; he considers himself the best of the best of men, the champion of the optimate cause and embodiment of the Republic," Titus added.

Many a time had the centurion witnessed Caesar roll his eyes, curse the stoic's existence or wryly smile upon hearing Cato being mentioned. He was renowned for his incorruptibility, his honesty and also his vehement opposition to Caesar and the triumvirate. Caesar and Cato had first famously clashed over the sentencing of the Catiline conspirators. Caesar had eloquently argued for clemency, yet Cato's forceful argument for condemning the guilty won out. The two men – the two unofficial figureheads of the opposing optimate and populares parties – clashed again over the reform of land rights. To help settle Pompey's legions Caesar passed legislation as consul to re-distribute the land of Cato's fellow patricians. Although the zealous senator often won the respect of colleagues for his integrity and sense of justice – all too often he was on the losing side in regards to Caesar and the triumvirate getting their way. He fought and lost his cause to root out bribery and end its power in deciding elections. He tried yet failed to prevent Caesar obtaining his governorship in Gaul. If Caesar would say it was day, Cato would call it night. Yet whereas Caesar now had his legions, all Cato possessed were words to champion his cause – and though he could be eloquent, he could also be obtuse and conceited. As Oppius had once heard Caesar joke, Cato would never use one word when ten could suffice.

"So you are the famous standard bearer? Yes, I have read the accounts of your heroic acts. My cook uses less garnish than the author of your deeds. Or should I call you the Sword of Rome? - A sword that Caesar would use to stab the heart of the constitution. You are of course just a mere soldier, not a philosopher or orator, but answer me this question standard bearer: are you a servant of Caesar or the Republic?"

His voice and words were measured, but underneath Oppius sensed that the stoical senator was as much a slave to his passions – and vanity – as most men. Perhaps more than most men. He was a dam that could break at any time. When younger, Oppius had heard about Cato nobly sharing the same conditions as the soldiers he commanded during his military service. Cato also battled to reform the cronyism and kleptocracy of Rome's bureaucracy. Yet the gnarled man standing before him now seemed but a shadow of the Cato of those stories. It seemed Caesar was not the only one who garnished the truth as much as Titus flavoured his dishes with garum. Before Oppius could reply Cato raised his hand.

"You do not have to answer. I know where your loyalties reside. I also have no desire to hear your lies. If I wished to fill my day with lies I'd read Caesar's colourful despatches from Gaul." Cato uttered Caesar's name as if brought a bad taste to his mouth, or was a curse.

Oppius here thought to himself how he would rather be filling his day differently, in the company of Fabia or a barmaid. Oppius thought about saying something, to either defend Caesar or just to let someone else speak, but the soldier had encountered politicians before. The sooner Cato finished what he had to say, the sooner he could be dismissed and get on with his life. Before he started to speak again however, he nodded to one of his slaves and his cup was topped up with wine.

"You think him a hero? A new Gracchus? Even should he wish to raise the people - or rather the mob – up, Caesar would still desire to stand atop of them and tread the mere mortals into the ground. Aye, even after all I am saying he will still remain a hero in your blinkered view of the world. But in the eyes of myself and the constitution Caesar is an outlaw and a war criminal. The governor of Gaul will not become a king of Rome. He must be brought to justice. I remember having to stomach the company of the dictator Sulla when just a boy. I would sit as close to him as we are close to each other now – and I vowed to myself that should I have been given a sword, I would have killed the tyrant then and there. More than the Gracchii your master desires to be Sulla. He is even more ambitious – and cynical – than Pompey. Caesar will be the death of the Republic, unless I can be the death of Caesar first. Yet I do not necessarily want to be the death of you, standard bearer. I do not doubt that you are brave but I would like to appeal to a love of reason and a love of the Republic – which hopefully still resides wuthin you. Or perhaps I will appeal to your survival instincts. You have been summoned here in order for me to ask you to pull out of your next gladiatorial bout. Caesar's Champion must sheath his sword. You can feign injury, or say you have been called back to Gaul, but you must instruct your sesterces-loving promoter that you cannot fight again. I will not allow Caesar to gain any more triumphs in Rome, even by proxy."

Cato's voice was now rough from wine and resentment. A film of sweat glazed his brow and the senator bared his teeth in a snarl when he mentioned Caesar.

"There is a good chance that I might be defeated. Surely then the triumph will be yours."

"There is more than a good chance that you will be defeated, should you face the opponent that Glaber believes you'll share the arena with."

Oppius raised his eyebrow and his face betrayed a fleck of surprise, that his opponent had already been chosen – and that Cato was in possession of the name before he was.

"You look a little shocked standard bearer. I know more than you might think. For instance I know about your fund-raising mission in Alesia and also how you tracked down and killed an agent from Rome in Britain, who was recruiting men to fight against Caesar in Gaul."

"I wasn't aware that was common knowledge," Oppius answered, steel replacing surprise in his expression.

"There is nothing common about the sum of my knowledge, standard bearer. I know that you are a hard man to kill."

The soldier was tempted to reply that his ex-wife had once judged him to be "a hard man to love", but he allowed Cato to finish.

"Therefore I would rather not leave anything to chance, as much as Glaber here posits that you do not stand a chance against your prospective combatant. Should you go ahead with the match however, then you will stand little chance of survival afterwards – no matter what the outcome. I can assure you of that. I will prove that you are a hard, as opposed to an impossible, man to kill."

10.

Evening.

A bulbous moon, assisted by a quartet of braziers, helped illuminate Titus Fabius' garden. Oppius sat alone on a bench, downed another wine and then re-filled his cup. After his meeting with Cato the centurion had found the nearest tavern. He was soon approached by the establishment's resident strumpet but he was not in the mood to raise a smile, or anything else, in relation to her advances. He just wanted a drink, or several. After an hour or two of attempting to drown his sorrows he headed back to the villa. Oppius slept off his bout of drinking and, when awake, found the nearest slave and asked him to bring a jug of wine to the triclinium. The centurion proceeded to give an account of his meetings with Mallius and Cato to his friends. Titus immediately instructed a couple of his attendants to visit some relevant contacts and discover the name of Oppius' mystery opponent.

As ever Titus was a generous host and all manner of dishes were laid before his guests. Roscius paid his compliments to the chef, although he bestowed even more compliments upon the slave who served him the food, Helena.

"She is a woman with great attributes," Roscius remarked to his host.

"Aye, I've noticed you've been admiring her attributes – both of them – all evening."

The joke did much to relieve the tension in the air, created by Oppius' news and dilemma.

At the same time as a course of fruit was brought out towards the end of the meal, one of Titus' attendants returned and whispered the name of Oppius' prospective opponent in his ear.

The colour drained from Titus' face and he briefly closed his eyes, as if praying that the news could have been otherwise.

His opponent would be the Sicilian, Decimus Baculus, Titus revealed.

"His nickname is "The Doctor", due to the clinical nature of his victories and his custom of retaining body parts as trophies from his defeated opponents. He sometimes wears a necklace, with fingers hanging from it. Mallius has been a snake again. Baculus isn't the best gladiator in Rome – that title belongs to Brutus Matius – but it could easily be argued that he's the second best the profession has to offer. The Doctor has killed more people than the pox – and the deaths have been just as agonising in many cases. He won his freedom some years ago. The optimates still employ him to come out of retirement every now and then though, when a gladiator gains favour with the populares and needs to be put in his place. He is fast, strong and vicious. He is also proficient with sword, spear, shield and dagger. His armour and arms are first rate. I have seen him kill – and kill easily – as a retiarius, secutor or murmillo. There would be no shame for prudence to defeat valour, Lucius, and for you to pull out of the match. Glaber is right in that you cannot be considered the favourite for the contest. Baculus will not look to merely wound you and have the crowd decide whether you should live or die. Or you may triumph, but still leave the arena crippled or disfigured. And from what Cato is saying, even if you win you will lose. Rufus Glaber is not a man to be toyed with. If Cato and the optimates unleash him, he will not hesitate in killing you should you survive the bout. I urge you to re-consider if you are still thinking about fighting, my friend. Caesar would understand. He can also doubtless think of alternative ways of extorting the list of names out of Mallius. The man is a snake, or insect, and Caesar can crush him as such."

The centurion merely nodded in reply, to convey that he understood and appreciated his friend's advice, but then just silently rose from the table, grabbed a cup and jug of wine and made his way out into the garden. Titus was about to say something, either in protest or support, but Roscius gently clasped his host's arm and shook his head. The legionary knew better than anyone when his centurion just wanted to be left alone.

"A rat caught in a trap," was how Glaber had described him, Oppius thought to himself. But rather the soldier judged others to be the rats, taking bites out of him. Feeding upon him. All of them – Mallius, Cato and even Caesar. If he fought then it would surely mean either death in the arena by Baculus' hand, or death just outside the arena by a dagger in the back from Glaber or one of his mercenaries. And so the easy option would be to pull out of any contest. Caesar would lose his intelligence, or at best be delayed in obtaining it. At least he would not lose a centurion. Mallius would lose money, but Oppius wasn't about to lose any sleep over that. Titus had argued that there would be no shame in refusing to fight. Better to lose one's honour than one's life. Yet the soldier could not wholly embrace such arguments. He recalled something that the young Fabius had said whilst the unit travelled to Rome from Gaul. The youth had quoted from his favourite poet after Teucer had asked what he was reading:

"Mine honour is my life; both grow in one;

Take honour from me, and my life is done."

It started to rain. The wind howled in the background, whether wildly or mournfully. Oppius heard a hiss and sizzle as spots of water fell over the hot coals of the braziers. He picked up his cup and jug and headed back inside to join his friends. Oppius forced a smile and clasped a fraternal hand on Roscius' shoulder. The unit greeted him with an apprehensive silence and forced themselves to smile reassuringly in return, albeit their expressions soon returned to being downcast.

"Don't look so glum. You're not at my funeral quite yet."

"What have you decided to do?" Titus asked, looking more apprehensive than most.

"We're going to head back to Gaul," Oppius replied. His host sighed in relief and nodded in support of the centurion's decision. "But not immediately. After all, I wouldn't want to miss my appointment with the Doctor."

11.

Gaul.

Caesar sat in the inner sanctum of his tent and adjusted the laurel wreath on his head. He wryly smiled, being reminded of a piece of graffiti in Rome that someone had recently reported to him. "Caesar does not want to wear a crown because he desires to be king, but rather because he wishes to conceal his bald head." Although slightly amused by the comment the satirist would be smiling on the other side of his face if ever Caesar found out who it was.

Joseph, Caesar's aged Jewish attendant, shuffled in at twice the usual pace of his doddering gait (his mind, or wit, however was as quick as any man's in the camp).

"This is from a messenger. Once he recovered his breath, he mentioned that it was urgent."

The general opened the message from Titus Fabius and read it intently, his expression conveying both intrigue and disappointment.

"How did your Solomon express it Joseph? "There is nothing new under the sun." It seems that Oppius has been loyal and Sextus Mallius disloyal, choosing to serve Mammon rather than Rome. The former shall be rewarded, whilst the latter shall be punished. Here, read this," Caesar stonily said and handed the letter to his man-servant.

"At least you could not ask for a better soldier, fighting as Caesar's Champion," the wizened attendant remarked after taking in the message. Joseph liked and admired the centurion, who had risen from the ranks. Unlike many of his master's officers and legates, who came from moneyed or aristocratic backgrounds, Oppius married a sense of duty to his position of power. Too many of Caesar's officer's were serving in the army in order to further their political careers – and in regards to their political careers they would ultimately look to take from the system rather than give something back. He could never envision Oppius toadying up to Caesar in order to vie for the position of collecting taxes in a province, or bidding to become a praetor.

"I agree. But even Lucius' best might not be good enough this time."

Caesar read the name Decimus Baculus again and shook his head, either in despair or disbelief. Caesar had recently purchased his own gladiator school (in the long term it would prove cost effective for him to possess his own gladiators, rather than pay someone else when financing a season of games during elections or a triumph). He had looked to hire the veteran fighter to train his new men, but was advised that Baculus was already in the employ of the optimates. Caesar's brow creased in worry and Joseph wondered whether his master's thoughts were dwelling on potentially losing his centurion, or on having his prestige tarnished should "Caesar's Champion" be defeated.

12.

It was agreed that Baculus would fight in the role of a hoplite. Oppius, again, would fight as a centurion.

"At least you might garner a few more cheers of support, fighting as a soldier," Marcus Fabius remarked to his commanding officer, trying to offer him a morsel of consolation. The friends were once again gathered in the garden. They were also joined by Roscius' cousin, Sergius, a former gladiator. The afternoon sun did its best to come out from behind clumps of pink-grey clouds. The smell of the freshly-baked bread before them warmed the air however.

"I wouldn't be so sure. The people are all for soldiers in a time of war, or immediately after a great victory, but otherwise they do their best to forget about us. They'll complain about the cost of an off duty soldier, pass by a crippled veteran whilst walking to the temple, or condemn his drinking or whoring," Oppius replied, with disappointment rather than rancour infusing his tone.

"Aye, I'll make you right. The people much prefer their soldiers conquering foreign lands, than a full local barracks bringing down the value of their properties," Sergius said. Sergius looked more like Roscius' brother than cousin, such was the resemblance between them. They shared the same large build, square shoulders and even squarer jaw. But even more so they seemed to possess similar temperaments. Sergius' nickname had been Hilarus ("The Cheerful") outside the arena, but Hercules inside of it. When he had first joined the party of soldiers earlier in the afternoon Teucer had asked Sergius about his history.

"I signed up as a gladiator after being found guilty of killing a man. I had a disagreement with a tax collector. He struck first, but I struck harder. I tried to knock some sense into him. Unfortunately I knocked the life out of him... Gladiator school was tough, but others found it tougher. I was already in good condition and could handle myself. Some were former slaves, some former prisoners and some were volunteers, looking to make their name or fortune... My first fight was nearly my last. I was seriously wounded by a Numidian who was as strong as Roscius' love of wine. But thankfully I defeated the savage. He sheathed a dagger in my leg. But at the same time I sheathed one in his neck... There are plenty of worse fates to that of being a gladiator. The food is good and regular. Some of my fellow gladiators knew how to have a good time and laugh, as well as knowing how to fight. There were plenty of loners and sullen brutes as well though... The crowd liked me. I pretended to like them back. Make no mistake - the mob can be as vicious and as merciless as any combatant. Victory brought certain bonuses, so to speak, however. The wife of a governor requested to "see my scars" one evening after a contest. She inspected my scars again the following night and I became her lover. In some ways I had to perform and exert myself more in her bedroom than I did in the arena. She also often hired me out to her friends, for them to inspect my scars too. But I don't want to complain. I was getting paid for something that I would have paid for. Eventually she even paid for my freedom and I bought a small farm just outside of Corfinium. I still, however, keep abreast of who is making a name for themselves in the arena."

"Never mind about the property prices coming down. How do we bring down this bastard Baculus? Does he have any weaknesses?" Titus exclaimed, re-focusing the group.

"I hear he has a weakness for blondes, but that's unlikely to be decisive in the arena," Teucer joked, albeit the group all but ignored the satirical Briton's comment.

"Baculus has few weaknesses. Indeed if I were given favourable odds I might even bet on him to defeat Brutus Matius – Charon – Pompey's prize gladiator. Baculus possesses stamina and speed, strength and skill in abundance. Yet you may have a chance if you frustrate him. Anger may provoke a mistake, although you'll still need to get inside the point of his spear to best him. Aye, if we can somehow heat his blood so he sees a red mist, we might blind him. But you'll need to be armed with Caesar's luck, as well as his steel," Sergius remarked, whilst arming himself with a cup of wine and slice of bread (before his cousin could finish off both).

"We'll still need to beat the point of that spear. How can we turn his main weapon into a source of weakness? I don't doubt that Lucius can use his shield to defend against the jab of the hoplite spear, but how can he then counter-attack successfully?" Titus buried his head in his hands due to being deep in thought, or despair.

"I have an idea," Teucer announced, with a gleam in his eye that didn't just come from the wine. His friends, this time, gave the archer their attention.

13.

"Will the Doctor find a cure to defeat Caesar's Champion?"

"Unlike lightning, can the Sword of Rome strike twice in the same place?"

So read some of the advertising and graffiti discussing the bout.

Rain slapped down throughout the early afternoon but it still could not dampen the spirits of the crowd inside the arena on the outskirts of Rome, which housed the much anticipated contest. The cheers – and laughter – had only recently subsided from the event which preceded Oppius' match. The promoter had organised a spectacle in which condemned prisoners were armed with swords and given special helmets, restricting their sight. Arena slaves then pushed them towards each other; the prisoners would slash wildly and look to defeat their opponents. The last man standing would gain his freedom. Bloodied corpses, some with their faces half cut off or their bowels hanging out of their stomachs, were wheeled past Oppius as he stood in the tunnel. He shook his head in disgust, lamenting the cruelty and waste. He could have made something of these men should they have been made to enlist in the army. But Rome had deemed them fit but for the charnel house. Blood and garum seemed to be the Empire's two most prevalent trades nowadays.

"Are you ready?" Titus asked, hoping that this would not be the last time he ever spoke to his old friend.

"As ready as I'll ever be. What are my odds?"

"Bigger even than the balls you've needed to go through with this."

"Should I not upset the odds today my friend I want you to make sure that my mother is provided for. Collect any payments from Mallius and Caesar that you need to."

"You have my word. But you make sure you defeat this bastard, otherwise I'll have my son read out one of his poems at your funeral. Good luck." Titus shook his friend's hand and departed, passing by Oppius' opponent as he did so. Both Titus and Oppius squinted slightly in the dimly lit tunnel – such was the polished gleam of the veteran gladiator's armour and weaponry. His breastplate and greaves were inwrought with silver and gold. Roscius could eat his dinner off the small hoplite shield, Oppius fancied – although Roscius could and did eat his dinner off any surface. The gleam from his helmet and shield could also temporarily blind an opponent in the afternoon sun, Sergius had warned the centurion. An attendant had even polished the gladiator's sandals. Should it be a fashion contest, then Oppius had lost already. He was an amateur to his opponent's professional. Decimus Baculus had dark features and a trimmed, black beard. He was slightly taller than Oppius – and his reach slightly greater, the soldier judged. His figure was an alloy of both strength and athleticism. Baculus was as well conditioned as any soldier he had encountered. There was an air of coldness and precision to the undefeated fighter. Sergius had said that "The Doctor" had a block of ice for a heart. Oppius had drily replied that his ex-wife had at least provided him with a sparring partner to deal with such an opponent.

The stone-faced gladiator nodded cursorily at his combatant and stood next to him. As he did so, Baculus tightened his grip around his long hoplite spear, his forearm bulging with muscle. He also twisted the spear so that the leaf-shaped blade caught the attention of his would-be victim. Oppius had seen many a spear-head before, albeit none so polished or recently sharpened.

Both men stood patiently next to each other as they heard the murmur of an announcer and a few bursts of cheers from the arena through the tunnel.

"I have read about some of your exploits in Gaul. You are a genuine war hero. It'll be a shame to kill you," Baculus said flatly. "You probably hoped that you would die upon some distant battlefield, clutching an enemy standard."

"Actually I hoped that I would die of old age in my bed, clutching a servant girl."

The veteran gladiator let out a grunt cum laugh.

"I have a cousin who serves in the Tenth in Gaul. He said you were a good officer, unlike most of the martinets or aristocrat's sons playing at soldiers that the army is filled with. You shouldn't be here centurion. I shouldn't be here either. I should be back home, with my wife and family. Yet still we remain puppets. Caesar pulls your strings. Cato has pulled mine."

"We could always cut our strings and agree not to fight."

For a moment Baculus paused and thought about the novel proposition. He wryly smiled but soon wanly shook his head.

"The stage is set and the audience are expecting a performance."

14.

A crescendo of sound greeted them like a blast of hot air from an oven as they walked into the arena. Baculus remarked to his opponent to try not to be distracted too much if the crowd called out the gladiator's name. Oppius could not quite tell whether he was intending to intimidate him, or if he was offering words of support. The roar of the arena eclipsed that of the rain. Again Oppius felt, at best, indifference towards the mass of bloodthirsty spectators – at worst he held them in contempt. He ignored most of the comments emanating from them, although he was amused by the odd one or two.

"Kill him... Shove his own sword down his throat... It's Greece versus Rome. The legionary will always defeat the hoplite... Send him back to Caesar in a box. Better still, in two boxes..."

Oppius gazed around the crowd to try and pick out where his friends were seated but things all blurred in to one rolling sea of faces and colour. However, due to their white togas – and designated area – the centurion could pick out where the senators were seated. Most were sat still, popping olives into their mouths – attempting to appear impervious and imperious compared to the animated crowd. Oppius wondered which ones were on Mallius' list and would be for or against Caesar in his bid to become consul again. Cato, his brow knitted together, gave the centurion a look of daggers; he looked as though he was chewing upon two wasps, Oppius fancied. He had failed to reply to Cato's numerous messages over the past day or two, which warned of the consequences of Oppius entering the arena again as Caesar's Champion.

Oppius also recognised the famous round face and distinct quiff of Pompey (it was rare for the First Man of Rome to leave his estate outside of the city and attend a gladiatorial contest, especially when his champion fighter "Charon" was not taking part). Time, or the tragic death of Julia, had aged him considerably since the last time the centurion had seen him. Caesar had once called his friend "a double-edged sword of charm and cruelty". Pompey the Great's original nickname, during his time under Sulla's command, had been "the teenage butcher". Both names had been earned. Age had not only changed his appearance though. The once dictatorial triumvirate had grown more conservative in his politics and sought the approval and love of the Senate, as well as the people, in recent years.

Finally, looking along the row of seats, Oppius spotted the odious figure of Mallius. One of his young slaves was fixing the pleats in his toga, whilst another filled his cup with wine. The merchant noticed the centurion, smirked and raised his cup to him. Oppius was tempted to reply by raising his own hand in a somewhat different gesture.

Cheers and rain swirled around in the arena. Thunder rumbled in the background; so did the low chant of "Bac-u-lus, Bac-u-lus". Clouds scraped across a marble-grey sky. At least the sun would not be strong enough to reflect off his opponent's armour or shield and blind him, Oppius thought to himself. The centurion wiped his hand on his tunic, not knowing if his palm was moist from sweat or rainwater. He drew his sword, breathed deeply and nodded to the umpire to convey he was ready. His heart beat fast, as if he was perched upon the transport ship again - about to invade Britain.

Baculus skipped swiftly and smoothly towards him, his spear jabbing out like a lizard's tongue. Oppius easily brought his shield across and sidestepped to deflect the blow. Immediately the soldier was impressed and wary of the gladiator's speed. Keep moving, keep surviving, Oppius told himself as Baculus stabbed the spear forward again, after the odd playful feint to do so. The centurion sensed that the gladiator was merely sizing him up, checking for any weaknesses in technique or fear in his opponent. The Sicilian had also satisfied his curiosity in regards to discovering that the centurion had reinforced his shield; it would take an almighty effort for him to punch through the scutum.

Baculus leaned back but then quickly skipped forward, stabbing low and then high. Parts of the crowd gasped with each offensive. Although heavier than the regulation legionary's shield it still appeared light on the soldier's arm and Oppius blocked both thrusts. The veteran gladiator nodded, either in appreciation or because the attack had confirmed something about the soldier in his mind. The centurion was growing a little anxious – solely defending – but he remained patient. Keep moving, keep surviving.

Sweat and rain chilled their faces. Baculus circled around his opponent, prey; sometimes he prowled, sometimes he almost danced. The voice of Tiro Casca, a veteran legionary, crept into Oppius' head. He would perhaps have castigated the gladiator with his mantra of "Stop dancing and start fighting" when teaching swordsmanship. Yet the soldier quickly shook off such idle thoughts, shaking his head as if there were cobwebs between his ears.

The gladiator probed and then sprung forward again. This time however Baculus' momentum took him much too far forward. Years of drilling meant that Oppius stabbed rather than slashed. His sword clanged upon the bright hoplite shield, but for the first time the centurion found himself momentarily inside Baculus' spear point. Oppius punched his own shield forward and knocked his opponent backwards. The gladiator soon regained his balance but a cheer of encouragement rang out around the arena for the underdog. The cheer was succeeded by the chants of "Cae-sar" and "Opp-i-us". Roscius, Teucer, Fabius – and dozens of other current and former soldiers who Titus had bought tickets for – led the chants of support.

Baculus seemed initially distracted, or disconcerted, by the dramatic change of support in the crowd but his aspect soon grew as steely and cold as the blade on his spear. He rushed forward again and unleashed a flurry of attacks. The jabs were more powerful, but less controlled. Oppius moved back and then sideways, so as not to get cornered against the sides of the arena. Keep moving, keep surviving he voiced beneath rasping breaths. To gain a brief respite – and put his opponent on the back foot - the centurion pretended that he was about to throw his gladius (as he had famously done so to defeat Aulus) but Baculus flinched not and merely raised his shield a little higher in precaution.

Again the hoplite gladiator launched another wave of attacks, sometimes feinting, sometimes creating new angles in which he stabbed his spear forward. Still the crowd chanted for himself and Caesar – which fuelled rather than perhaps diminished Oppius' chances of defeat, he fancied.

For once the centurion's defensive technique was flawed and with a flick of his wrist Baculus altered the trajectory of his spearhead and it sliced through Oppius' unguarded thigh. The soldier stumbled backwards but remained on his feet. More changeable than the weather, the crowd gasped – and then ominously began to chant "Bac-u-lus" again. Perhaps the chanting this time had been led by Oppius' ex-wife.

Blood dripped over and darkened the sand. The centurion witnessed a hint of a smile – a triumphant smile – upon the gladiator's face. In nine bouts out of ten Baculus would have bested Oppius. But it was just this one bout which mattered. The Sicilian sensed victory. But so did his opponent. Oppius would use his injury to his advantage, pretending to be more wounded than he actually was. He hobbled backwards and raised his shield up higher, as if cowering before the superior fighter. His actions bred an even greater confidence in the gladiator. The Doctor could afford to be less clinical. The crowd smelled blood – and defeat – too. Cato could afford to look more stoical and indifferent in regards to the outcome, believing now the result would be in his favour.

It was time to roll the dice and gamble on Teucer's plan. Baculus moved forward. Oppius retreated, sluggishly. The gladiator could almost afford to toy with the soldier, like a cat would with a mouse. The spear was jabbed forward again. Oppius however moved quickly, deliberately, so that the tip hit – and slid through – a designated part of his shield. Teucer's idea, in order to disarm Oppius' opponent of his spear, was to cut and disguise a slot in his scutum. The spear head would be suddenly, unexpectedly, trapped and Baculus would be left temporarily vulnerable.

Once his spear was caught in the vice of the shield Oppius moved his arm out to further unbalance his opponent. Baculus, although caught unawares, still instinctively brought his small shield close to his stomach and chest but the shield was too little and it was too late. The centurion stabbed his sword down fast and hard into the gladiator's thigh, twisting the blade when he reached bone as he did so. Baculus howled in agony; the unholy sound could have woken the gods. The gladiator stumbled backwards fell on the sand. The blackness of unconsciousness nearly swallowed him up but the veteran warrior still instinctively drew his sword as he lay upon the ground. As soon as the blade had left its scabbard though it was flying through the air, as Oppius kicked it from his hand. Baculus, in the last throw of the dice, weakly threw his shield at the centurion but the soldier easily deflected the missile with his scutum.

The crowd erupted in a thousand cheers, or just a mighty one. If the sound had woken the gods then Oppius hoped the gods would punish them for the disturbance. Roscius and his unit didn't even need to prompt the chanting of their officer's name. In time to the calling out of "Opp-i-us" the bulk of the crowd jabbed down their thumbs, instructing the centurion to finish off the wounded gladiator. The rain and sound of the crowd swirled around him more violently as Oppius stood over and looked down at his stricken opponent. The once triumphant smile had been washed away. The blood too had drained from his face. Baculus closed his eyes, either in resignation or a final prayer. He opened them again on hearing the chants of "Opp-i-us" turn into a chorus of boos and hisses. He gazed up to see that his opponent had sheathed his sword and was raising his arm – and thumb – up to the crowd. The centurion had of course been tempted to raise his hand in a somewhat different gesture to the mob in the arena.

"I would kill you, if I was standing there," Baculus said, emotionlessly.

"I know. Cato – and my ex-wife – would have rewarded you handsomely for it as well."

"Caesar has a worthy champion."

"Caesar has Caesar. He doesn't need me. Nor should you need Rome. You fought well, but go home to your family and retire. Kill time rather than people."

The hint of a smile came over the gladiator's face once again.

Mallius smiled so widely it looked as though his grin was wrapping itself around the whole of his head. Already the merchant was thinking about how he could entice or blackmail Oppius to enter the arena again. Perhaps he could even fight – and defeat - Pompey's champion, Charon.

15.

At least Mallius had arranged for a coach to take him back to Rome after the contest, even though the coachman was slightly confused at first, as he believed that his passenger would be going by the name of Baculus. Titus and his unit would make their way back on their own.

The muscles in his injured leg both throbbed and tightened at the same time as he rested in the coach. Mallius provided his own surgeon, who had once been in the employ of Crassus, to attend to his wound after the bout.

"I must look after my prize asset," the merchant explained, before leaving to check upon ticket receipts.

As the surgeon stitched up his wound Oppius received an unexpected visitor. Pompey stood before him in a gleaming white toga and ran his hand through his hair, attending as much to his famous quiff as to the centurion. Pompey smiled gently, although his hard eyes struck a hard note compared to the softness of the rest of his face. He initially just surveyed the soldier, without uttering a word. He stared intently, as though he were almost taking in the soldier's past, present and future as well as his physical appearance. At the same time as feeling that he was the centre of Pompey's attention, Oppius also felt that he was but of vague secondary importance to the senator; a lesser mortal (if indeed Pompey considered himself wholly mortal).

"You fought well centurion. You are a credit to the army. Although it seems that Caesar's Champion possesses Caesar's good fortune, it also seems that Julius has infected you with his weakness for clemency. Should you have somehow been in a position to spare my gladiator, Charon, he would have despised you all the more and murdered you in your sleep afterwards. As much as you have won a battle, you have not won the war," Pompey exclaimed, sneering a little as he mentioned the words "Julius" and "clemency". Before Oppius could reply – although he was at a loss as to how to – Pompey took his leave.

Sunlight finally melted through the clouds and rain as Oppius entered the city, though dusk was about to melt the day. Mallius had arranged for a litter but Oppius never felt comfortable travelling in them. They were for over-indulged women, or overweight patricians. He walked gingerly, but made his way through the streets towards Titus' house. Oppius was mindful of his injury – and also watching for Rufus Glaber and his men. He spotted one not before long, just as Oppius was about to enter a small fruit market. He was wearing the same distinctive white toga, bordered in black, from before. The soldier soon saw two more. As he looked in their direction they averted their glances. One pretended to buy some grapes whilst another bent down to re-fasten his sandals. Yet Oppius still couldn't see Glaber. He would want to be here to finish the job, the soldier suspected. This was one of the few opportunities when the centurion would be isolated and vulnerable.

Night slowly moved in, as did Glaber's men. Oppius moved as quickly as he could, his crutch clacking upon stone, away from his pursuers. Sharp twinges of pain ran up and down his wounded leg. There was an argument for staying in the crowded marketplace, but it would be all too easy to receive a blade in the small of his back in such an environment, he judged. Blood trickled down his thigh from his wound opening up as he walked briskly down a side street. The side street turned into an alley. The alley turned into a small courtyard. Yet the courtyard was a dead end. Its entrance was also its exit. The courtyard was made up of three high stone walls. Overhanging the walls on one side were balconies from an apartment block. Even if uninjured, the walls were too high for him to scale. Oppius turned around – and finally saw Glaber.

"I would say that you're a lucky bastard, given your victory earlier, but given your situation now, I'm not so sure," the mercenary said - relishing having captured his quarry so easily. With a movement of his head he instructed the two random citizens in the courtyard to depart. They did so without protest. He was flanked by two pairs of his men either side of him, and two of his men stood guard behind. Oppius instinctively moved backwards, ending up not far from the graffiti-filled back wall of the courtyard. Glaber's unit looked capable, if unexceptional. There were six of them. In his condition he would just about be able to defeat two of them, at best.

"I bet against you and lost money on the bout. I'm not happy Lucius. Cato is also unhappy." Glaber drew his dagger. The clouds bound themselves together again, shrouding the city in the dullest of lights.

"He should learn to bear his lamentations with fortitude," Oppius drily replied, reciting the philosophy of the stoic.

"You shouldn't be so hard on Cato. He suggested that I only go so far as to prevent you from ever fighting again. But I argued that I needed to be more thorough. Partly because if I don't end things for you now, you might end things for me later. Ideally I would have liked to make you suffer – blunt the Sword of Rome – but we are where we are. You are where you are. A rat caught in a trap."

"You're right. But I'm not the rat – and you've not set the trap."

Teucer and Marcus Fabius appeared from out of one of the apartments and stood on a balcony above the courtyard, their bows drawn. Titus and Roscius appeared at the entrance to the courtyard, blocking off any possible retreat by Glaber and his men.

"Ideally I would have liked to have made you suffer, but we are where we are. You are where you are." Oppius drew his dagger.

Enraged and desperate Glaber sprang forward and made to attack the centurion but Teucer's arrow caught him in the chest and knocked him off his feet. Marcus Fabius felled the enemy in his sights too. Roscius and Titus made short work of the two men closest to them. Roscius swung his elbow into the face of his enemy, breaking his nose. Blood then blurred his opponent's vision – and he saw not the legionary punch the gladius into his chest. Titus' opponent blocked two of his sword strokes, but he did not block the third. The former centurion moved in close and buried his sword up to its hilt in the mercenary's stomach. The remaining enemy received arrows in their backs as they looked to retreat and attack Roscius and Titus standing at the mouth of the courtyard.

"Have mercy," Glaber pleaded, as he looked up at the centurion.

"I'm afraid I used up all my clemency in the arena," Oppius replied – and then buried the bottom of his crutch into the mercenary's eye-socket. Titus and Roscius slit the throats of the wounded. Their white togas, with black trim, were now awash with blood.

"Thank you," Oppius remarked to the approaching Titus.

"No need. I should be thanking you my friend. It's about time my sword was covered in blood again, as opposed to just rust."

Teucer and Marcus Fabius jumped down from the balcony and retrieved their arrows, as if plucking them out of the dead from a battlefield in Gaul. The men looked around at the courtyard littered with corpses and just nodded to one another.

"Can we go eat now?" Roscius finally asked, ending the eerie silence.

16.

Oppius woke and squinted in the light of the early afternoon sun the following day. In the distance he could hear the sound of a cohort being drilled outside the city walls. He suspected they were raw recruits, being broken in. Even if they were doing everything perfectly the legionary in charge would still find fault and drill them again. He may even drill them once more, just to amuse himself. The raw recruits' reward would finally come when they could drill a future batch of raw recruits and amuse themselves accordingly.

Oppius and his own unit had feasted well the night before. They turned in early however, tired from the day's events. Roscius worked his way through various courses before leading the servant girl Helena off so he could have his "dessert". Titus also retired and went to bed early, explaining that he had to run an errand in the morning.

Titus returned to the house as Oppius sat down to eat a lunch of bread, pork, olives and figs.

"We have been grateful for your hospitality Titus but I think it's time we moved on. Instead of another one of your banquets I must have a home-cooked meal, in my mother's kitchen," the centurion explained to his friend.

"I understand."

"Before I leave Rome however, I must first call on Mallius and retrieve the other half of the list for Caesar."

"I already have the full list in my possession. He would have broken his promise again and forced you into the arena. For all of his wealth, the only money he needs now is for the Ferryman. I bloodied my sword one more time. Suspicion will fall upon his two young slaves, who I paid off and instructed to leave Rome immediately. Few will mourn the death of a banker, especially one who was owed so much money by so many people."

"Will Cato not be suspicious? And how much should I worry about him coming after me, for defying him and killing Glaber and his men?"

"Cato has far too much pride to consider that a mere centurion could merit being his enemy. He is far more obsessed with battling and defeating Caesar, to the point where he will even join forces with his former enemy Pompey to do so. No, out of sight means you will also be out of mind. As well as the list, I must also give you some letters from Octavius to pass on to Caesar. Marcus visited the boy again this morning."

"What does he think of him?"

"Marcus was impressed by his intellect and good manners. He thinks that Octavius will be a student rather than a soldier though – a poet rather than a politician."

"You may have once said the same about Marcus. Perhaps Octavius will surprise a few people too."

"We'll see. Time will tell – far more accurately than any augur. I trust that you will return to Rome soon my friend. You are always welcome at this house. I hope that this visit has not put you off returning, although I wouldn't blame you if you kicked the dust from your shoes in regards to the city. You've been thrown into the arena twice to be slaughtered – and you've seemingly made more enemies than a tax collector whilst here."

"It could have been worse."

"How so?"

"I could have bumped in to my ex-wife."

Both men grinned and decided to drink one last jug of wine before Oppius departed.

End Note

Special thanks also to Amy Durant for helping to put this book together.

For the most part I like to think I have remained true to the spirit and facts of the real history behind Augustus: Son of Rome and the Sword of Rome series. However, I have perhaps been a bit unfair and used dramatic licence in my portrait of Cato in this book. To redress the balance I can recommend reading Plutarch's Life of Cato (indeed it would be remiss of me not to recommend reading the whole of Plutarch). "Rome's Last Citizen" by Rob Goodman & Jimmy Soni may also be of interest. Should you be interested in reading more about gladiators then Philip Matyszak's "Gladiator: The Roman Fighter's Manual" is a fun and fact-laden starting place (it also provides a list of further reading at the back).

Sword of Rome: Gladiator is a work of fiction. In short, I have made stuff up. Any historical accuracies, unwitting or not, are my own.

Thank you to everyone who has written to me about my books. Your emails are always welcome. Please do let me know should you have enjoyed this book, or others. I have been particularly touched by your letters regarding the novel Warsaw. It took quite a bit out of me to write it. I'm glad it has been able to give something back. I hope you also enjoy the enclosed bonus story of Raffles: Bowled Over.

I can be reached via richard@sharpebooks.com

Lucius Oppius will return in Sword of Rome: Rubicon

A Brief Affair

1.

Rome. 25BC.

Morning.

Sunlight poured through the window of his bedroom, gifting an attractive sheen to the woman's already burnished flesh. Rufus Varro woke, stretched and gulped down a large cup of water, dehydrated from last night's wine.

He heard, in the distance, a couple of carters arguing about their right of way into the street. Neither wanted to give way. The merchants were soon trading insults.

"Cocksucker!"

"Eunuch!"

It was unlikely that the two men would ever be close, if the names they were calling each other were anything to go by, Varro mused. In the distance he could see smoke belching out of the tanneries and bakeries, casting a pall over parts of the city. The nobleman imagined how the populace would be stirring and scurrying along the capital's narrow streets like insects, going about their business. Slaves would be attending to endless onerous duties. Wine vendors and costermongers would be setting out their stalls in the marketplaces. Bleary-eyed drunks would be staggering in or out of taverns. Brothel owners would be kicking out any customers, who had paid to stay overnight. Senators would be rehearsing their speeches, like actors, in front of the mirror, enamoured with the sound of their own voice. They needed to make sure that their policies -

and insults towards rivals - were as polished as the marble statues of Augustus which populated Rome.

The alluring woman lying next to him, Sabina, stirred too. Varro considered how the wife of the tax collector, Valerius Glabrio, seemed comfortable and accustomed with waking up in a different bed to her own. The same claim could be made for the priapic aristocrat and poet himself. Even if Varro wasn't so hungover, he would have had trouble remembering the number of lovers he had woken next to over the years (during his time being married, or otherwise).

"Satisfied?" she whispered - or purred - lasciviously, rubbing her shin against his.

Varro breathed in her aromatic perfume, smiled at his new mistress, clasped her hand and kissed her fingertips. As he leaned over to pour out a cup of water for the woman, with his back towards his lover, he yawned.

"Satisfied doesn't come close," the handsome nobleman replied, donning an enamoured expression again.

"Will you compose a poem for me? I want you to immortalise me."

"I'd love to. As long as you do not consider me unfaithful for spending time with my muse instead of you," Varro said, suppressing his instinct to roll his eyes and cringe at his response. He briefly thought about which of his previous poems he could adapt, with minimal effort, to dedicate to the woman. The aristocrat had been part of a generation of poets that considered itself the heir to Catullus. Certainly, Varro drunk as much as his idol. He would spend his evenings at dinner parties hosted by his distinguished neighbours on the Palatine Hill - or the poet would descend into the Suburra to drink, gamble and whore the night away. It had been some time since the "new Catullus" had composed anything of note. Rufus Varro was no longer a poet. Rather, Rufus Varro was a spy.

2.

A day before spending the night with Sabina, Marcus Agrippa summoned the agent to his house. The palatial property had once belonged to Pompey the Great and then Mark Antony. To the victor, the spoils.

Varro was shown to the consul's private chambers. Whilst the recently named Augustus led the armies of Rome on the Spanish frontier, Agrippa had been charged with governing Rome. Caesar's lieutenant had helped win the war, on land and sea, against Mark Antony. Now he was helping to win the peace. As well as managing the grain supply, commissioning various building projects (including new aqueducts, temples and public gardens) and attending to administrative duties to help run the empire - Agrippa also oversaw a network of spies. Sometimes wars are fought in the shadows.

Less than a year ago Varro assisted Agrippa in uncovering a coup against Caesar. He became, in the spymaster's words, "an asset". The reluctant agent had been recruited for other assignments since. Espionage was an essential weapon in the war against the enemies of Rome. It was also a tool to help the aristocrat fight against the enemy of boredom. Augustus himself had recruited his services for certain assignments. The demigod was not someone to say no to, Varro sagely decided.

Oil lamps hung from the ceiling. Maps of the empire adorned the walls. Marcus Agrippa sat at his desk, which it appeared might soon collapse from the weight of all the parchment, scrolls and wax tablets strewn across it. The consul buried himself in his work, feeling that he owed a duty to both Rome and his close friend. Although Varro believed that work was also a means for Agrippa to escape his grief, from the death of his wife, Caecilia. He had since, at the request of Augustus, married Caesar's niece, Marcella. The decision to take another wife had been borne out of duty to his friend, rather than from any love for the young woman.

A flicker of a smile animated Agrippa's stony expression, as Varro stood before the second most powerful man in the world. Caesar's lieutenant had a reassuring air of resilience and honour about him, like a war horse. He was as straight and efficient as a Roman road, as sturdily built as a Roman column. When he said he was going to do something, he did it - which was rare for a politician, in any age. Agrippa still preferred the company of soldiers to senators and often yearned to be back combating enemies on the battlefield, rather than dealing with the nest of vipers in the Senate House.

"I have an assignment for you, Rufus," Agrippa remarked, without preamble.

Varro sighed to himself, but not with relief.

"I will do my utmost to conceal my excitement," Varro said sarcastically, thinking, however, that sarcasm was the lowest form of sarcasm.

"There is no reason why you should know the name Valerius Glabrio. Glabrio oversees the collection of taxes for the area in and around Patavium. I recently received a couple of complaints about the administrator, accusing him of embezzlement and extortion. However, these testimonies are filled with rumour rather than evidence. Tax collectors are not known for collecting friends. The two merchants who have written to me may bear a personal grievance against Glabrio. Merchants are not known for their honesty and integrity. Should the case come to trial, any half-decent advocate would be able to discredit the witnesses. I do not wish to undermine the authority of our tax system and its administrators by bringing false allegations against Glabrio. But I cannot discount these allegations either.

"I want you to get close to Glabrio's wife, Sabina. Find out what she knows. We need to create a picture of his income and spending, in both Rome and Patavium. I am reliably informed that Sabina is a great beauty - and far from chaste. I'm confident that you will be able to extract the necessary intelligence from her. She will be attending a party, hosted by Lucius Tedius, tomorrow evening. Tedius tells me that Valerius will be absent, attending to his latest mistress. I am sure you're capable of seducing her, or letting her seduce you," Agrippa remarked, whilst glancing at the latest plans to refurbish a temple on the Quirinal Hill. Multi-tasking.

"You may be overestimating my charms."

"And you may be underestimating them. I'm confident that you'll get the job done, one way or another, Rufus. The assignment shouldn't take too long. It will be a brief affair, so to speak... But tell me, how's Manius?" Agrippa said, asking after Varro's bodyguard. The former gladiator, from Britannia, was usually at his friend's side.

"He's happily married, if there is such a state of being. As a belated wedding present, I arranged for Manius and Camilla to spend some time at my villa in Arretium."

"I can assure you that there is such a state of being, albeit it may seem like a brief affair too," Agrippa remarked, picturing his first wife, as opposed to second. "But it's as rare as a courageous Gaul, garrulous Spartan, honest politician or cheerful German. The German sense of humour is no laughing matter."

3.

The wine and conversation flowed at the party, hosted by the senator Lucius Tedius. Patricians and their wives, or mistresses, were out in force. The room was a kaleidoscope of colour and rustling, Chinese silk. Sapphires and amethysts, adorning alabaster necks, sparkled like stars. Serving girls re-filled wine cups and brought around silver trays laden with the latest, fashionable delicacies: octopi in mushroom sauce, spiced cubes of ostrich meat, sea bass infused with saffron and stewed apricots. Melodious harps played in the background. Outside, in the garden, a fire-eater and juggler made spectacles of themselves. Tedius had spared no expense, although, thankfully, their host had failed to arrange a mime to entertain his guests, Varro mused.

The aristocrat saw an old friend, Gaius Macro, and asked him to pick out Sabina.

"Are you on the hunt tonight then?" the former poet, now property developer and inveterate gossip, asked.

"A man needs his sport," Varro replied, burdened by his reputation, as opposed to proud of it.

"A married man needs his sport too. Unfortunately, my wife has ruined my evening again by insisting on coming along tonight. Instead of being hurled from the Tarpeian Rock, Rome should just compel its enemies to marry, as a punishment. You were right to divorce and regain your freedom."

Varro forced a smile, whilst experiencing his own sense of grief as he thought about his former wife, Lucilla. He had lost the only woman he had ever loved. Ever would love. Yet Lucilla was right to divorce him, to be free of him. Even before Varro became a spy, he was duplicitous.

The agent spotted Sabina across the crowded room and duly pretended to be entranced, enamoured. The wife of Valerius Glabrio was indeed a great beauty. Kohl-black tendrils of hair framed an olive complexion and sculptured features. Her pouting lips were ripe for kissing. Her V-necked gown showed off a diamond pendant, as well as other assets. Sabina stared at the handsome stranger, appreciatively.

"I don't suppose you know anything about her husband?" Varro remarked to Macro.

"I have met him on a couple of occasions, which were two too many. Glabrio is fond of talking about money. He would probably sell his own mother - and put her up for auction to obtain the best price - if he thought he'd profit from the deal. I have known poets to be less arrogant too. By all means cuckold the odious official."

Varro had every intention of doing so.

"It seems that you have already had plenty of hopeful - and hopeless - would-be suitors engage you this evening. I'm not sure which to class myself as, but I was wondering if you would take pity on me, as someone who is attending the party alone, and let me keep you company? My name is Rufus Varro."

The woman smiled, and even seemed a little coy. But not too coy. Varro also noticed a glimmer of recognition in her eyes as he said his name. Sabina had indeed heard of him. One of her friends had slept with the famous (or infamous) nobleman and poet, a year ago. "He was a fun and passionate lover… I hoped to unlock his heart, or his treasury, but we soon grew bored with one another," her friend remarked, tinged with regret.

Sabina eyed the handsome poet up, as if assessing the value of a statue. She had once sat as an artist's model and been sculptured. She fancied how the poet might be able to immortalise her in verse.

"I am Sabina. I have come unaccompanied too. My husband is devoting himself to one of his mistresses this evening," she tartly remarked. What is good enough for the goose is good enough for the gander, Sabina judged.

Varro continued to talk to the woman. Agrippa was right to state that she was a great beauty, although he failed to mention how she was no great wit. Despite her statuesque figure most of his jokes still went over her head. He feigned interest in her life, whilst wheedling information out of her. The reluctant agent was also an accomplished one. She mentioned how her husband had bought the tellingly expensive diamond pendant around her neck, that it had originally been a gift from Caesar to Servilia. The elaborate gold earrings hanging from her ears had once belonged to Cleopatra. Glabrio may not have showered his wife with too much time and attention, but he did shower her with gifts. Varro was all too aware of the exorbitant expense of maintaining both a wife and mistress.

Whether the desire-fuelled look in her eyes was borne from the wine, or lust, the agent didn't much care. The hunter had snared his prey. The party began to thin out. Sabina accepted Varro's invitation to come back to his villa. It was a short trip to travel across the Palatine Hill. A few of the litter bearers smirked, as they heard the noises the woman emitted behind the curtains. But they had heard it all before. Sabina also gasped on witnessing the size of the aristocrat's house. More than one mistress, over the years, had swooned upon realising how wealthy the poet was.

4.

Sabina beamed with delight, and then kissed the poet in gratitude, at the news that he would compose a poem especially for her. Hopefully her friends would be bitterly jealous. When she planted a second kiss on his lips, she slid her hand beneath the bedsheet. The woman was insatiable, Varro thought to himself. But there were worse traits a lover could own. One was having an irate husband, trying to bash down your door.

Fronto, Varro's wizened estate manager, calmly knocked on his master's door and conveyed that the lady's husband was currently at the front of the house, along with a couple of his attendants. Fronto had seen it all before. Usually Manius had been present, however, in such circumstances. The bodyguard had been proficient over the years in dealing with any unwelcome callers.

Varro gazed at Sabina with genuine concern, her aspect now filled with fear rather than lust. Her burnished flesh somehow seemed paler. A wave of dread crashed against Varro's heart too as he remembered Cassandra. The fate of his former mistress still haunted him. Her husband had tortured and murdered his wife, after she helped to uncover his plot to overthrow Caesar.

All was not lost, however. Varro instructed Fronto to hide Sabina in the wine cellar. As much as his slaves might be tempted to do so, they were not to confront Glabrio's bodyguards. Varro would lead their unwelcome guests away from the house.

Varro's heart was beating, but not with ardour, as he dressed and climbed out the window. He soon heard Glabrio cursing his name at the gates to his house. He called the aristocrat any number of names - bastard, coward, degenerate. Varro fleetingly thought how it would be difficult for him to find an advocate who could successfully argue against any of the tax collector's assertions.

Glabrio stood at the tall, iron gates to the property. The official screwed-up countenance was flushed, either from anger or the wine from the night before. He barked and growled, threatening violence on a whey-faced slave if he didn't let him in. Glabrio was close to ordering his bodyguards to rip the gate off its hinges or clamber over it.

The wronged - and wronging - husband still clasped the note he had received that morning, after coming home from spending the evening with his mistress. The sender stated he wished to remain anonymous - but he owed a duty to Glabrio to write to him. The letter informed that his wife had left the party last night with the aristocrat Rufus Varro. The sender had also overheard Varro malign Glabrio throughout the evening, how he couldn't afford to keep his wife in the lifestyle she deserved. He was just "a provincial bureaucrat." The nobleman made a boast of turning the official into a cuckold - and writing about the affair in a poem.

Glabrio's blood was quickly brought to the boil and he ordered his bodyguards to accompany him, as he marched through the streets of Rome in order to confront the ignoble aristocrat and collect his whorish wife. The tax collector would not have his dignity and authority impugned. He riled, as he imagined the laughter, from friends and enemies alike, should they read a satirical verse about the affair. Glabrio would deal with his wife accordingly. But first he would deal with the arrogant, upstart poet. He would have his attendants beat him - and he himself would thrash Varro, like he was an errant child, for his transgressions. The tax collector would of course wait until his bodyguards could hold his victim down, before metering out the punishment.

Glabrio witnessed a figure climbing over the garden wall and rightly suspected it was Varro. As he reached the top of the wall he glanced back at the gate. The bodyguards were ex-soldiers or ex-gladiators. Their tunics were stretched across their muscular bodies. Violence was a way of life. They were probably kept busy, guarding the unpopular tax collector or bullying and extorting money out of people.

Varro and Glabrio locked eyes. The latter's snarl turned into a wolfish grin. There would be no escape for the dissolute poet. Glabrio smelled blood. The hunt was on.

5.

Sweat dripped from his brow, his lungs and thighs began to burn, as Varro raced through the streets of the Palatine. He frequently looked back to chart the progress of his two pursuers. Although the bodyguards were large, they were far from lumbering. They were slowly and surely gaining ground, like an incoming tide about to drown him. He even began to hear the sound of their sandals slap against the paving stones.

At least the first part of his plan had succeeded. He had drawn the assailants away from the house. Fronto, Sabina and his slaves were safe. He just needed to get through the day with his bones intact. Varro cut through a few narrow alleys and descended into the bowels of the Subura. He was starting to tire. His legs nearly gave way, twice, as he ran along a cobblestoned street. Varro darted around a corner, into a high-walled courtyard. As he turned back towards the entrance, he was confronted by the two bodyguards, Hanno and Pollux, forming a human barrier to trap him on all sides. They panted, like hounds, and drew their cudgels. Varro was without his dagger.

Perhaps he was too exhausted, or frightened, to take on the brutal looking Hanno, whilst his confederate retraced his steps and fetched his master. Varro waited, his head bowed down like a condemned man awaiting a guilty verdict. A gust of wind kicked up some dust in the courtyard. The temperature dropped, but that wasn't necessarily the reason why a chill ran down his spine.

Glabrio's ire was replaced by an air of triumph when he witnessed how forlorn the aristocrat appeared. He imagined that the satirical poet had mocked him, in front of his wife, last night. But who was laughing now?

"I hope this will teach you a lesson. There is nothing that a man can take, that a tax collector cannot take back. Including his wife. I have encountered your kind before. You noblemen think you are entitled to everything or everyone."

The official was relishing his ability to sneer at and punish someone from the privileged classes, who had once haughtily looked down their noses at him.

"Sabina doesn't love you," Varro exclaimed.

Glabrio laughed, before replying.

"Ha! This shows how much poets know about love. Sabina's my wife, she's not supposed to love me. She is only supposed to obey me, which she has failed to do - and will pay the price. Everything has a price."

"If everything has a price, will you allow me to buy my way out of this? Can we not negotiate a settlement, for me to purchase my freedom? I would also be willing to pay you, so I can still see your wife. I am a man of considerable wealth. I can ensure Sabina is kept in a style deserving of her beauty. Surely, as a tax collector, you do not possess the means to give her everything that she wants?"

Glabrio laughed again, even louder.

"You might be surprised by how much I earn. And I have earned my wealth, instead of merely inheriting it, like you. At my villa in Patavium I have a personal treasury, which would rival yours. Corruption is rife across the empire, as plentiful as the air we breathe. We bid for the opportunity to collect taxes. It is only natural and just that we should pay ourselves a bonus for our work and investment. I have more money that I know what to do with. Because I have other people's money."

"Is that enough?" Varro asked.

"What do you mean, is that enough? Man is man. We always want more. And I will take more," Glabrio argued, creasing his face in either contempt or confoundment.

"He wasn't talking to you," Marcus Agrippa remarked, appearing from over the wall. "That will indeed be enough, Rufus. Thank you."

A couple of archers flanked the consul, training their bows on the dumbstruck bodyguards. Their barrel chests were no longer puffed out in confidence. A group of praetorians blocked the entrance to the courtyard, forming a human barrier. Ire replaced the tax official's air of triumph. The smile fell from his face, as swiftly as an executioner's sword plunging down onto a neck.

Varro breathed a sigh of relief. His plan had worked. The agent had been the author behind the anonymous letter to Glabrio. As they had pre-arranged, Fronto had sent a slave to deliver the message, once the estate manager had seen Sabina accompany his master back to the house. Varro, who was all too familiar with the neighbourhood of the Suburra, had deliberately led the bodyguards into the courtyard. To seemingly trap himself. Given the arrogant, boastful nature of the official - he was more conceited than a poet - Varro hadn't found it too difficult to prise a confession from his target. The fish had taken the bait.

As if Glabrio's testimony wouldn't damn him enough, Agrippa would soon give the order for his house in Patavium to be searched. The official's wealth would be appropriated by the state. It was unlikely that the extorted and embezzled monies would be returned to the bureaucrat's victims. Render unto Caesar what's Caesar's. Agrippa would ensure that Glabrio would not punish his wife for his own transgressions. He would also warn the tax collector against being tempted to exact any revenge on Varro. The agent had enough enemies to contend with already.

The affair - the brief affair - was over.

A Knight's Tale

"Christians, hasten to help your brothers in the East, for they are being attacked. Arm for the rescue of Jerusalem under your captain Christ. Wear his cross as your badge. If you are killed your sins will be pardoned."
Pope Urban II.

***

A chorus of belching, bravado, gossip, curses, dice-throwing and retching noises swirled around the weathered tavern, situated close to the docks in Taranto. The establishment was populated by various tradesmen, sailors, soldiers, and whores. The ale, wine, and a watery stew flowed. A barmaid's rump was slapped by a balding, drunken priest. A merchant haggled with a bored looking harlot, as he angled for a discount. Laughter rang out as the ruddy-faced landlord, Gotto, told a joke about a three-legged donkey, a fishmonger's wife and a blacksmith's rusty poker. Gotto could see the humour in most things. A couple of patrons laughed more than most, hoping that their host might reward them with a complimentary drink. Lamps were lit as the light faded outside.

Such an environment was a home from home for Edward Kemp, a veteran English knight. He downed another ale and nodded to a serving girl to fetch another round of drinks—before yawning and then contributing to the chorus of belching. His leather jerkin was as filthy as the joke Gotto had just told. Patches of grey had started to mark his stubble, beneath a broken nose and red-rimmed eyes. Edward couldn't quite decide if he was war or world weary. He drank too much (although he would argue that he drank just the right amount) and slept too little. The knight had spent over two decades fighting various campaigns across the continent, for various companies. Some led by lions, some by lambs. The cynical soldier had experienced enough of Christendom to know that God was about as real as dragons. Certainly, God and a protective dragon were absent when his parents had been butchered, by a Norman raiding party, during the Harrying of the North. Afterwards, the orphan travelled south to become a stable hand, then squire—and then a sword for hire, as a trained knight.

Edward sat in the corner with his long-term friend and brother-in-arms Owen, a stocky Welsh archer—who could be frequently found with a drink in his hand and a grin on his roguish face. The bowman ran a sharpening stone over an arrowhead, attached to its shaft. The two men had recently been joined by Loffredo of Ravenna, a knight who served in Bohemond of Taranto's company. Edward had previously served in Bohemond's army too. The famed and fearsome Norman prince, who had spent most of his life at war (whether fighting against the Byzantine Empire or his own brother), was keen to recruit the English knight once more. And so he had instructed Loffredo to track down the veteran, "If he's not in one of the taverns in town then he's probably dead in a ditch somewhere," and petition Edward one last time to join them on their armed pilgrimage. To capture Jerusalem.

Edward had already heard the news concerning the historic campaign several times. Soldiers and civilians alike were yammering on about little else. Pope Urban had given a sermon, a call to arms, at Clermont, for the noblemen and knights of Christendom to journey east and liberate Jerusalem from Turkish rule. The borders of the Byzantine Empire were under threat. Urban claimed that the Turkish hordes were moving westward, intent on conquest and enslavement. Turks were reportedly cutting open the bellies of merchants, as they travelled to the Holy City, to steal any coins they may have swallowed. Christians were being forced to convert to a heathen religion—and being disembowelled or burnt alive if they refused. Christian women were being molested and murdered. Even children were being slaughtered. Shrines and churches were being desecrated, smeared with blood. In return for their military service Urban promised the knights and noblemen that their estates would be secure in their absence. They would be granted a remission of sins. There was also the unspoken promise of booty. The pilgrims would be rewarded, in heaven and on earth. Word spread, like wildfire, about the crusade. Powerful magnates such as Raymond of Toulouse and Robert of Flanders committed their armies and resources. A bishop named Adhemar was hailed as the spiritual leader of the endeavour. Edward was far less zealous about the campaign. Should the Byzantine borders be threatened, then let the Byzantines defend them—or pay others to defend them, as they had done so in the past. When the crusaders reached the Levant—*if* they reached the Levant—they would be far from home. It would be difficult to call up reserves or provision themselves. "It was a fool's errand, a holy fool's errand," Edward had remarked to Owen, on more than one occasion.

Loffredo was all too aware of the Englishman's lack of enthusiasm for the venture. He had already mentioned his desire to return to England, not travel further away from the sodden island. Nevertheless, he still delivered his pitch. Bohemond would reward Loffredo if he could succeed in recruiting the doughty knight and skilled archer.

"Pope Urban is offering crusaders a remission on their sins. The Kingdom of Heaven awaits those who will serve the cause," Loffredo proffered. It would be a just war. "Thou shalt kill Muslims," could be considered a new commandment.

"I am more interested in how Bohemond will reward me in this life, than how God will in the next," Edward replied, after taking another swig of his ale, his voice as rough as his stubble. The knight thought how God would not be able to have his accustomed day of rest, given how many sins would be committed by the goodly Christians during the campaign—and he would have to forgive them.

"Bohemond instructed me to say that he is willing to negotiate terms," Loffredo said: "Only mention that I may be prepared to negotiate if you think that our fish isn't biting," the nobleman had briefed his agent.

Edward displayed little interest still in what Loffredo had to say, but the seed of the idea was taking root. For the past five years or so the Englishman had promised himself that his next campaign would be his last. His ambition was to sail back to England and live a quiet, comfortable life. To buy a house and a share in a tavern. He had spilt enough blood over the years, for three lifetimes. He quite literally had the scars to prove it. But as much as the crusade may be a fool's errand, it might be equally unwise to not profit from it. A fool and their money are easily parted. If Bohemond wanted to open-up the purse strings to recruit him, he wasn't about to argue with the magnate. Edward certainly would not be joining the campaign out of a sense of Christian duty. *The Almighty doesn't much care for me—and I don't much care for Him either.* The campaign could just make it to Constantinople and turn back, in all likelihood. The various princes would probably fall out with one other—or run out of food. It could be easy money—which, aside from free money, was the best kind of money. There were worse commanders out there to serve under too, Edward judged. The Norman prince had inherited his father's guile—and knew how to win. Bohemond also knew how sage it was to look after his men off the battlefield, so they would look after him on it.

"Tell Bohemond that I am prepared to listen to any new terms. He can purchase my soul for nothing, but my sword arm doesn't come cheap," the Englishman replied, raising his voice over the increasing din of the tavern. The regulars had started to enter. A trickle became a stream. A few more whores descended the stairs, dressed in cheap jewellery and either cheaper garments. A trio of dockhands, with besmirched faces, ordered the first of many drinks. Edward recognised the men from previous sessions spent in the tavern. The knight expected to see at least one of the dockers asleep in the gutter, in a pool of piss or sick (or both), by the end of the night. A couple of well-built, well-armed figures also entered and sat on adjacent table to Edward. They both glanced around the establishment, decidedly unimpressed and disdainful. Owen thought that they looked like they were sucking on a lemon and chewing a wasp simultaneously. Their complexions were sunburnt and freckled. They shared the same lantern jaw and mane of fire-red hair. They were probably brothers, or at least cousins. They grunted a couple of times, but otherwise spoke quietly to one another.

"I will tell him," Loffredo replied. "I hope you change your mind, Edward. Jerusalem and our Christian brethren need liberating. God wills it. Do you just want to spend your days in run-down taverns, drowning your sorrows and tupping second-rate whores?"

"Aye, I've found my promised land, Loffredo. And I have got nothing against you finding yours, in the desert," the Englishman remarked, good humouredly. Edward offered to buy his fellow knight another drink, but he took his leave. Bohemond had instructed the agent to seek out other soldiers to recruit. To take the cross. To save or damn them.

***

Owen placed a jug of ale on the uneven table and sat down on his even ricketier stool. Before wending his way through the crowd, back to Edward, the archer caught the eye—or she caught his eye—of Maria. The young, but experienced, whore was wearing a red linen dress which tantalisingly hung off her left shoulder—enticingly displaying the promise of her right breast. Owen had already spent two nights with Maria. Ever since she had offered him a small discount after their first encounter, he had become veritably smitten with the lissom, Venetian brunette.

"It looks like I may be joining this crusade, to Jerusalem," the Welshman remarked to Maria, his muscular arm bulging, from holding the large jug of ale. "This might even be the last night I spend in Taranto, for some time."

"Well make sure you spend it with me," Maria replied, before pouting, her voice even sultrier than usual. "I'll ensure that you set off on your campaign with a smile on your face, instead of a pox between your legs—which will happen if you visit the neighbouring brothel. The girls there are unclean. Foreign. I will even give you another discount, because I like you and I may never see you again. We'll have some fun, I promise."

"You've made me an offer I can't refuse. I will see you later in the evening, I promise," Owen assured her, his eyes and other parts of him bulging, before making his way back to the table.

A short silence ensued after the archer sat back down, as both men started to ruminate on the possibility of joining the crusade.

"It seems that Bohemond has become a servant of God," Owen finally, wryly, remarked, arching his eyebrows—a picture of devout scepticism.

"Bohemond probably looked into the possibility that God could become a servant of him first. I will listen to any fresh terms he offers, before making a decision to pledge to the cause," Edward said, responding to his companion's unasked question.

Owen trusted the knight to negotiate his pay too. More than Edward, Owen needed the coin that the crusade could provide. He had experienced too much good living recently, if "good" meant sinful, in the form of gambling, drinking and whoring. The bowman wondered what the women in the East would be like. He had heard a disconcerting rumour that Muslim fillies didn't drink, which would limit the archer's ability to take advantage of them. He worried that there must be a reason why so many women from the East wore veils too. Was it to conceal an ugly truth? He joked to himself that he would aim to bring back a chest of veils for the women of Wales, to make them seem more appealing.

"Our Count of Taranto may well submit to God's will, but I can't envision him taking many orders from fellow mere mortals. He has grown accustomed to being in command, since his father passed," the bowman remarked, whilst keeping half an eye on Maria. She was flirting with a dockhand. He was in his cups—he might soon be in her bed.

"Aye, but the likes of Raymond of Toulouse have grown accustomed to being in command too. I would back Bohemond to be the dog who gets the bone, after any fight, though. The Count of Taranto tends to get what he wants. He's an ambitious bastard. Too ambitious. He won't be happy until he's sitting on a throne somewhere, with no more kingdoms left to conquer. Even then he would find something wrong. His food would be too cold, his wine would be too sour—and his wife would be too faithful," Edward argued, refilling his cup.

"He will surely have to swallow his pride and submit to the will of Emperor Alexios. Not that Alexios would consider himself a mere mortal."

"I suspect that Bohemond will be willing to align himself with the Emperor, right up until the moment when he stabs him in the back. Unless Alexios stabs Bohemond in the back first. At some point the Emperor will regret inviting our paymaster into his alliance—letting the fox into the hen house. Bohemond would happily chew him up—and spit him out. It's natural for a son to want to carry on the war that his father lost, although Robert Guiscard did disinherit Bohemond. Alexius is no longer as strong as he once was. Hence, he needs us to fight his battles for him. The empire is contracting. The Seljuk Turks are a pack of hyenas, bringing down a once mighty lion. Alexios used to be an accomplished general. But court life has made him soft. Rumour has it that he spends more time with his mistresses, than his generals and advisers. He's as pox ridden as a French harlot. He is more likely to raise taxes than morale nowadays. The Byzantines are not known for their loyalty and honour. Alexios will have plenty of close allies, waiting for him to fail. He's just keeping the throne warm for them... The fight has gone out of Komnenos. His eunuchs have bigger bollocks."

The sound of a couple of chairs scraping across the floor drowned out the noise of Owen's laughter. The two hulking figures from the neighbouring table now towered over the Englishman and Welshman. Riled. Glowering.

The atmosphere suddenly changed, as if a chaplain had just extinguished all the candles in his church.

"Curs! Your words are tantamount to blasphemy. You are not even worthy enough to voice the Emperor's sacred name. You would be executed for such calumny and sedition in Constantinople. We are Varangians," the slightly larger of the two men, Gorm, asserted—he widened his nostrils and puffed out his chest whilst pronouncing the name of the Emperor's famed unit of bodyguards.

His companion, Sten, grunted or growled in agreement, his hand clasped around the hilt of a large, curved dagger.

The Varangian Guard. Their reputation preceded them. And was deserved. The ancient group of soldiers was more akin to a cult. Formidable in battle. Fiercely loyal. Their ranks were largely made up of Norsemen, although many Anglo-Saxons migrated to the East and swelled their ranks after William the Conqueror's victory in 1066. Or, as Edward and others called him, William the Bastard. The Varangian Guard seldom recruited soldiers from inside the Empire, to lessen the possibility of corruption and treachery. Few troops could live to tell the tale of standing against the elite soldiers. Their large battle-axes could chop down men, as easily as a gardener can pull up weeds. The Varangians were instrumental in defeating Robert Guiscard's forces, snatching triumph from the jaws of defeat during more than one engagement. Bohemond still cursed the imperial guard whenever their name was mentioned, although his antagonism was tempered with admiration.

The Varangians had been ordered by Tatikios, one of the Emperor's key generals, to travel to Taranto to deliver orders to a Byzantine spy posted there. Tatikios was keen to assess the strength of Bohemond's forces, before they descended upon Constantinople, along with the other crusader armies. Both Gorm and Sten were seemingly in competition with one another, as to who could project the most imperious and contemptuous sneer when looking down at the westerners. They were long time companions, kinsmen from the same tribe. Their fathers had served in Harald Hardrada's army. After Hardrada's defeat at Stamford Bridge, the spearmen had taken their families east. The sons followed in their father's footsteps and served in the Varangian Guard, swearing oaths of allegiance to Alexios Komnenos.

The sight of the Varangians would have intimidated most men. But Edward Kemp wasn't most men. The knight had no desire to enter into a fight with the men in front of him, but he couldn't—wouldn't—withdraw from any encounter either. It was not a question of being brave, rather the Englishman would not be bullied. He sized up the taller of the two Varangians in front of him. His face was large and brooding, like a bullock's. His chest was as broad as a double-headed axe. If they all drew their blades, blood would be spilt. Lives, as well as pride, were potentially at stake. And victory was far from certain.

Edward calmly got to his feet. Owen stood too. The knight took a swig of his ale and spoke with held his hands up in a conciliatory gesture.

"We meant no offence. Can I buy you both a drink?"

The knight offered an olive branch. But it was snapped in two.

"No. But you can get out of our sight. Leave!" Gorm spat out.

Edward turned to his friend. Owen offered up the subtlest of nods, to convey that he would be ready if things went from bad to worse.

"We will soon be allies, gentlemen, fighting together in the East. We need to learn how to drink together under the same roof."

"We do not need you or Bohemond's army to triumph in the war with the ignoble Turk," Gorm posited, disgusted by the thought of the Varangian Guard despoiling its honour by having to fight alongside the likes of the barbaric English knight in front of him.

"Your precious Emperor has decreed that he needs us—and I thought you considered him infallible, like our venerable Pope Urban," Edward drily replied.

"Our loyalty is to the Emperor and Empire. Your crusader armies and your Pope Urban can go rot. You are English, no? England can go rot too," Gorm argued, bristling, as he echoed the words of his late father in relation to the accursed island.

"I'll drink to that," Owen chirped, smiling as the Welshman raised his cup in a toast.

"Are you mocking us?" the dog-toothed Sten emitted, his voice as rough as granite. The brawny Varangian looked like he wanted to kill the archer. Which he probably did.

"You're doing a great job of mocking yourself. But I'll help you out if you want," the feisty bowman replied. As much as the Emperor's bodyguard were renowned for their sense of honour, their sense of humour was conspicuous by its absence.

Sten let out a grunt cum growl again. The tension in the air increased, like the tightening of a garrotte. The Varangian gripped his dagger even more, pulling the weapon out a little so a slither of the blade was showing.

"I'd leave that dagger in its sheath, if I was you," Edward warned, his voice now as cold, flat and hard as his sword. "You might do yourself an injury. Or rather I'll do you an injury."

Perhaps part of Edward knew that the Varangian's temper would boil over, as oppose to simmer, by issuing the threat.

An indignant Gorm spat out a curse in his native tongue, or an order for his anxious companion to attack. Edward and Owen had participated in more than one tavern brawl over the years. The knight was aware that chivalry had little part to play in proceedings.

Gorm reached for his sword, but as he grabbed the weapon Edward buried his boot into his opponent's groin. Pain clanged upwards through his torso, as if the blow might cleave him apart.

Owen reacted as quickly as his friend—and fought just as dishonourably and desperately. The Welshman first threw the contents of his cup into Sten's face, with his left hand. And with his right he snatched up the arrow he had been sharpening from the table and plunged it into the Varangian's eye. The arrowhead easily pierced through the jelly—and halfway through what little brains the Dane possessed. The high-pitched scream, which sounded like the cry of a eunuch (while he was in the process of becoming a eunuch), sliced through the convivial atmosphere of the establishment. But then the noise subsided, as abruptly as it started.

Gorm staggered backwards, doubled over in agony. Winded. The air rushed out of his lungs, like bellows. Just as he was about to recover—and his fingertips tickled the hilt of his sword—Edward repeated the assault. The dockhands winced, and their eyes nearly watered in sympathy as the blow landed. Gorm's tree trunk-like legs buckled and he fell to the floor, like a drunk. The Englishman towered over the prostrate Varangian. A brace of rats scurried along the floor behind Gorm and disappeared into a V-shaped hole. Edward had no desire to proffer a pithy line—or make a display of triumphalism over his opponent. He took no—or very little—pleasure in killing the Varangian. The Dane drew in a breath and was about to speak. He might have wanted to plead for his life—or condemn the Englishman. Before any words fell from his drooling, twisted mouth, however, the knight stabbed the point of his sword into the Varangian's gullet. He gurgled and writhed for a few moments, then stopped. Tavern brawls could be, like life, nasty, brutish and short. The imperial bodyguard was not the first man Edward had ever killed in such a manner. And he probably wouldn't be the last.

Mouths were agape. Whispers scurried around the tavern like the rats, or like air rushing around the inside of a seashell. Gotto could laugh at most things. But not everything. The landlord pursed his lips, either upset at the needless loss of life—or that he would have to clean up the mess. The Englishman and Welshman drank a lot and were usually no trouble. But (nearly) no amount of money was worth such trouble. Word would spread about the incident faster than a pox spreading at the neighbouring brothel.

Edward could not help but observe the landlord's displeased expression. He would give Gotto some coin by way of an apology for the trouble he had, not caused, but been involved in. His host would be responsible for scrubbing the blood from the warped, wooden floor. But it would ultimately fall to Bohemond to sweep things under the carpet. Edward knew he would be in the prince's debt. And Bohemond knew how the knight would repay him. *The Count of Taranto tends to get what he wants.* The Englishman probably would not be able to now refuse his request to join the foolish campaign. And his bargaining position to negotiate upwards was as dead as the Varangian with blood still pouring out his throat. The knight would still petition for Owen to receive an increase in pay, however.

Edward sighed. He was world and war weary, he realised, as he wiped the blood off his blade—using the Varangian's shirt to do so. It was a shame that he had to kill the man. It was equally a shame that his fine boots were a couple of sizes too big for the knight.

Owen liberated the curved dagger from the corpse at his feet. Not to serve as a trophy, but to sell on and use the money to spend another night with Maria.

"What will happen now?" the archer asked his friend.

The Welshman was going to joke that they could use a remission of sin at present. He was also going to mention how he wanted to test himself against the famed Turkish bowmen in the East.

"God knows," Edward replied, emitting another sigh.

Raffles: The Gentleman Thief

Acknowledgements

I would like to thank Emily Banyard and Helen Ng in particular for helping Raffles: The Gentleman Thief come to fruition. I would also like to thank Saul David and Patrick Bishop for their support over the years. And last but not least, thank you to all the Angels (you know who you are).

I hope that any devoted fans of the Hornung stories can forgive my re-boot. Should this story have been your introduction to the character of Raffles however then I urge you to read the original tales – and become a devoted fan too. A similar statement and request can also be made in regards to the readers of Conan Doyle and the original Sherlock Holmes stories.

Raffles and Harry "Bunny" Manders will return in Raffles: Bowled Over.

Chapter One

A tendril of smoke gracefully swirled up from his cigarette into the low-lying, jaundiced fog. Jermyn Street was cast in such a gloom as to be worthy of a scene from Dickens – or Dante. Yet despite the noxious atmosphere – and the gelid air misting up my breath – I could still divine, like a lighthouse in the fiercest storm, the twinkle in my companion's eye. Oh that incomparable, incorrigible, twinkle that had acted as a Siren song – seducing me and nearly dashing me upon the rocks of prison – these recent months.

"We have had stranger jobs, more dangerous jobs and most decidedly more profitable jobs, my dear Bunny, but I warrant that there have been none so local," Raffles wistfully expressed whilst extracting his trusty skeleton key from the inside pocket of his navy blue woollen blazer.

I briefly considered the proximity of our first 'job' together on that fateful night in Bond Street on the Ides of March, but then nodded in agreement. We were but a few minutes from the Albany, where Raffles resided (when he was not visiting country estates and scoring runs during the day at cricket, and scoring loot at night as a gentleman thief – or I should rather say *the* gentleman thief).

"The ice may not even have melted in your gin and tonic Bunny, by the time we return," Raffles buoyantly added.

The clip-clop of horses and the thrum of a carriage's wheels approached and then rescinded. A party of late-night revellers, either heading to or from a club, could also be heard in the background. With his skeleton key, lifted from a porter at Browns Hotel, Raffles unlocked the back door to Hatchard's of Piccadilly.

"If knowledge is the key to everything Bunny, then this pick-lock runs it a close second," Raffles remarked whilst holding up the skeleton key as it glinted – along with his aspect – in what little light the street offered.

I tightened my sweaty grip around the handle of the black carpet bag which carried the tools of his trade (or rather *our* trade). I then gulped and forced myself through the door, which Raffles courteously held open for me. Fear slithered up and down my spine like an eel. I thought of a thousand things that could go wrong. Even after all this time Raffles had to be confident and courageous enough for the both of us, which thankfully he was.

We soon came through to the back of the shop. I lit our lamp with a match, still trying in vain to noiselessly do so as Raffles could. Tables and shelves of books warmly glowed before us, the gold and silver leaf upon the spines shimmering in the amber haze.

"There are riches here Bunny worth more than those housed in Aladdin's cave," my companion whispered in awe, his eyes feasting upon piled-up volumes of classic titles by Walter Scott, Edgar Allen Poe and Balzac. Raffles was as well-read as he was well-dressed. One was much more likely to find him reading an edition of Byron or Pope than pouring over the society pages or cricket scores even.

A presentiment came over me however, as my gaze found itself inexplicably drawn to a solitary copy of *Crime & Punishment* squatting upon a table – and I cursed the day that I ever set foot across the threshold of 221b Baker Street.

Chapter Two

My heart froze – and then beat like the clappers – as I held the card in my hand.

'*Mr Sherlock Holmes requests the company of Mr Harry Manders at 221b Baker St at the earliest opportunity.*'

There was an authority in the bold script that transformed the request into a command. The message had been delivered by a wiry, sandy-haired street urchin – no doubt he was a member of Holmes' renowned gang of Baker Street Irregulars. The imp barely disguised his amusement at my perplexed – or just plain terrified – reaction. My face turned as white as the card I was holding and I almost had to ask the youth to lift my jaw up from the depths to which it had dropped. I rubbed my eyes and read the note again, hoping that the burgundy and late night at the baccarat tables were playing tricks upon my mind. A part of me even fleetingly fancied that Raffles might be playing a prank. But this wasn't his style. Also, I knew him to be away. He had been invited to play a game of cricket in Truro. "Normally, I wouldn't play in a match that is so late in the year – but the wish to bowl out the son of our host and then take out his daughter has persuaded me," Raffles explained. "Suffice to say I will not need your assistance for this excursion my friend. The only thing I wish to steal this week is a young woman's heart – and perhaps her virtue," he playfully stated, with a Mephistophelian gleam to his expression.

The ruddy-faced urchin continued to look amused – and expectant.

"Mr Holmes doesn't like to be kept waitin' for a reply mister," the boy eventually piped out, his Cockney accent reminding me of the one Raffles sometimes employed to conceal his true background and breeding.

I was here going to assert that it was presumptuous of Mr Holmes to think that anyone or everyone should drop what they were doing for the day to attend upon him, but I was somehow compelled – or condemned – to reply that I would be able to meet Mr Holmes' request and arrive at Baker Street around noon.

The messenger nodded and thanked me – and then scampered away before I could question him further as to the import of my imminent appointment. I returned to my study and finished off composing an important piece of correspondence, my hand trembling as I signed my name. I tried to commence to write an article, but to no avail. I was far too distracted by the morning's events (and by how the events of the afternoon might unfold). My mind was ablaze with curiosity, but more so worry. Was the game afoot – or game up – for Raffles and I?

Chapter Three

Unable to sit still or concentrate – and wishing to get some air – I decided to leave early and walk to Baker Street. Dr Johnson was perhaps correct in surmising that, 'when a man is tired of London, he is tired of life.' Yet although London is seldom dull, it can often be irksome. Albeit the sky was a vast, oceanic blue but with wisps of cloud breaking up the azure – the scene below the firmament was less serene. Gaudy dresses, shrill voices, equine excrement and seven shades of grime assaulted the senses upon Regent Street. Ill-dressed and ill-mannered tourists conspired to vex me by walking at a slow, obstructive pace – and often travelling upon the wrong side of the pavement. Most of the women out shopping were overdressed and underwhelming, with even the less affluent appearing to have more money than sense. Such was my anxious mood that I resentfully wished to myself that even more of them could discover the joys and freedom of the bicycle, and totter off to the countryside to leave me free to get to Baker Street more expediently.

I pulled my jacket around me tight to trap the warm air in and also to prevent the advances of pickpockets who populate our capital, like vermin must have, during the great plague. I would encourage all gentlemen to put mousetraps in their pockets when shopping along Oxford and Regent Street. I am not sure if this advice may seem hypocritical or ironical given my profession, but mousetraps may do more to stifle petty theft than any well-meaning legislation put forward by our Liberal Party. Oh, if only such devices could snap off the fingers of the taxman too (that far more scurrilous and destructive thief). A hat tax, a window tax and a death tax! What next? Will they soon tax us just for journeying in to London?

I travelled along Oxford Street, marvelling at the number of ribbon-strewn window dressers at work, busily changing over their displays in light of the forthcoming festive season. I thought to myself is it me, or is the lead up to Christmas getting longer each year – as our society inexorably slips into serving Mammon instead of God?

I decided to cut through Marylebone. Similar to Bond Street, the prices and intimidating wealth of the area tend to leave the pavements less congested. I sighed and rolled my eyes at witnessing the queue of slack-jawed tourists and our own lower middle-classes snake out of Madame Tussaud's waxwork museum. Marie Tussaud, when alive, created wax figures of the likes of Voltaire, Jean-Jacques Rousseau and Benjamin Franklin. Yet what mediocre and vulgar personalities now populate the museum. I once overheard an eminent social commentator express that 'the exhibits in Madame Tussaud's hold up a mirror to our society.' If so, we should verily be ashamed.

Upon turning into Baker Street I nearly bumped into an esteemed cabinet minister and his companion. Raffles and I had recently encountered the couple at a party (or, for us, it was a job). The cabinet minister was, of course, too important to remember me – or even to apologise to me as he nearly mindlessly knocked me over. I smiled however, upon recalling Raffles' comment at the party in relation to the couple, 'If that is his wife, he should get a mistress. If that is his mistress, he should return home to his wife.'

And so I came to 221b Baker Street, having failed to wholly distract myself during my walk, from the dread I felt at being summoned by the nemesis of every cracksman and criminal in London. I told myself that I could, like Raffles, act a part and be on my way. Yet in the interim of ringing the bell and the door being answered I gulped down two large breaths of free air, in part believing that they could be my last for a while.

Chapter Four

A middle-aged lady with a matronly manner and slight Scottish burr to her accent led me upstairs and into a large sitting room. I am practised at being in the company of very important personages – and in regards to Raffles I am practised at being in the presence of greatness – but nothing could ably prepare me for being casually introduced to –

"Mr Sherlock Holmes and Dr Watson."

Even if I had not been a cracksman's accomplice I would have still stood sheepishly, guiltily, before them I warrant.

A faint, acrid smell of chemicals peppered the air. The curtains were part drawn across the large windows to slash half the room in light and half the room in darkness. I raised my eyebrow and startled a little at seeing a cluster of bullet holes pock-marking the William Morris wallpaper at the far end of the room (Raffles might have satirically argued that the bullet holes improved the pattern). Books, papers, clothes, scientific apparatus and a violin also populated the chamber in a certain ordered chaos. Portraits of Linnaeus and Newton (a not inconsiderable detective himself during his prosecution of the gentleman forger William Chaloner) hung above the fireplace.

Dr Watson hung an elbow upon the fireplace and cleaned out his pipe. He was dressed smartly, but not ostentatiously, in a tweed suit. A stolid Rugby player's build could still be traced beneath some middle-age spread. He smiled at me and I immediately picked up upon his avuncular character – friendly, trustworthy and not a little unwise.

"Thank you for attending upon us so promptly Mr Manders."

The head-masterly voice – or it had the richness of an actor's perhaps playing a headmaster – shot through me. Although the greeting was cordial, I still feared for my life (or at least my liberty). The world famous detective sat, or rather was slumped, in a worn leather chair. A tower of newspapers and a coffee table, besmirched with all manner of stains, flanked the chair. Albeit nigh on midday, Holmes was still in his dressing gown. His frame was tall and languid, although there were occasions during our meeting when his body suddenly became as taut and alert as a pointer's. He had a coffin-shaped head and sharp eyes which, unlike his lanky body, were never at rest. His nose was indeed hawk-like and protruded out to such an extent, that I fancied Sherlock Holmes could have smelled tomorrow. His slender fingers were steepled together and his focus seemed to be directed upon wrestling with an abstract problem, as well as dealing with me. Just before he was about to speak again the clock upon the mantle chimed twelve. Holmes and Watson here wordlessly turned to each other and nodded. Watson proceeded to pour two glasses of sherry. There was a sense of familiarity and routine to their behaviour that was akin to an old married couple. Watson offered me a glass but I declined. After pausing slightly, savouring the first sip, Holmes turned his attention to me again. Those two large eyes seemed like shotgun barrels and this Bunny awaited his fate.

Chapter Five

"Now we both know Mr Manders, that I could have you arrested for several counts of burglary."

I gasped and was about to protest my innocence, ignorance and indignation when Holmes just merely shook his head and waved his hand to convey that my protestations would not be worth the effort. I turned my head to the door behind me – and my eyes darted around the rest of the room for any possible escape route should I need one – but Holmes just smiled and shook his head again.

"Please, Mr Manders, There will be no need for flight or fight. If I wanted to put you behind bars I can assure you that you and Mr Raffles would be playing baccarat, using the currency of cigarettes rather than sterling already. Indeed you and Mr Raffles are two of the least likely people I would like to incarcerate – at this present moment in time," Holmes added, looking at me askance as he uttered the last part of this sentence.

"How…how did you guess?" I stammered, infinitely more perplexed and terrified than I had been earlier that morning, upon receiving my summons.

"I never guess. It is a shocking habit – destructive to the logical faculty!" Holmes replied, his body jolting upright in his seat and his tone suddenly reproving. He soon relaxed again however and wryly uttered, "You know a conjurer gets no credit when once he has explained his trick. But suffice to say, a couple of newspaper reports of certain thefts and cricket matches in the same vicinity pricked my interest in Mr Raffles. Inspector Lestrade supplied me with some additional information about the robberies – and then one of my Baker Street Irregulars shadowed Mr Raffles for the day to confirm my suspicions. Thankfully, for you and your friend, I have bigger fish to fry as the saying goes – and I always believed that I would have more use for an amateur cracksman, such as Mr Raffles, this side of the walls of Newgate prison. And it turns out I was correct in that judgement. Besides, my inquiries lead me to believe that Mr Raffles' heart is in the right place – even if the valuables of certain grand families that you and your friend have stayed with are not. Most of those grand families have committed acts of larceny as to make your heists seem venal by comparison however. I am too aware of Mr Raffles' clandestine donations to charity from the fruits of his labours. I also know you to be this Robin Hood's John Little, Mr Manders. Or perhaps you are more so his Alan-a-Dale, recording Mr Raffles' exploits much like Dr Watson here acts as my Boswell?"

I nodded a little and smiled, feebly, to convey to the detective and Dr Watson that his suspicions were, again, correct. I tried to retain my composure but I could feel my heart race and the vein in my neck throb. I wafted up a vague prayer to God in Heaven that all would be well – and also sent out a prayer to Raffles in Truro to come and save me.

Instead of my deliverance though, I was furnished with an offer that I couldn't refuse.

Chapter Six

"What I am about to tell you, Mr Manders, is confidential. It is meant for your ears and those of Mr Raffles alone. You both seem to have the capacity for discretion, given the double lives you have led over recent times. Two days ago my brother Mycroft stood in the very same spot that you are currently occupying. It is rare for my brother to leave his rooms at Pall Mall or his sanctuary in the Diogenes Club, so I was expecting that the reason for his visit was of some urgency and importance."

I could not help but notice the detective's body tense up a little when speaking of his brother, as though his very name could get his haunches up. Dr Watson continued to scour out his pipe and smile at me kindly, as though I were one of his patients. I certainly began to feel like a victim.

"You are a writer by day I believe Mr Manders. We have already deduced your nocturnal vocation. Therefore, I take it that you are familiar with the French author Alexander Dumas and his popular tome, The Three Musketeers? For my part I am unfamiliar with such potboilers. I find the plots to be overcooked and the characters contrived."

I here noticed Dr Watson roll his eyes a little in embarrassment and exasperation, and I recalled a line from one of his books, A Study in Scarlet, concerning the philistinism of his friend. '*His ignorance was as remarkable as his knowledge. Of contemporary literature, philosophy and politics he appeared to know nothing.*'

"There is a character, one Rene d'Aramis, contained in the novel's pages. As well as being a Musketeer, this Aramis, based upon a genuine historical personage, served as a spy for the

French government - and his brief, whilst over in England one summer, was to ingratiate himself into certain circles of the aristocracy. He was able to do so through ingratiating himself into the bedrooms of various wives and mistresses in society. He was, like your Mr Raffles, a gentleman thief albeit he looked to steal state secrets rather than mere trinkets."

Holmes again looked askance at me, barely disguising his contempt for the common criminal he was addressing.

"He was also, like you Mr Manders, a writer. He kept a journal of his exploits whilst serving over here. He also kept a number of compromising letters written by his conquests. This journal and these letters were given to a lover he was particularly fond of it seems – a mere grocer's daughter rather than duchess – for safe keeping. One of the letters contained in the packet is especially compromising to a current member of our government, as it questions the parentage of one of his antecedents – and therefore brings into question his legitimacy. This letter has recently fallen into the hands of a well-known journalist whose motto is "the truth will out." Before the truth can do such a thing however, it must first be sold to the highest bidder. A newspaper editor – who is a fellow member of the Diogenes Club and who was doubtless an under bidder for the document – brought the issue to my brother's attention. For Mycroft and his Ministry the truth is something to keep in a strongbox, rather than air, like dirty laundry. I must confess that I am indifferent to the fate of the aforementioned minister, but my brother called in a marker and asked me to resolve the situation. I have been charged with retrieving the letter and destroying any provenance of the allegations. Mycroft and his fraternity can be seen to take no part in the affair. I too, am loath to concern myself too much with this trifling matter. I am not my brother's seeker. So I am charging you and Mr Raffles with resolving the situation. I believe that the phrase is considered to be that of 'passing the buck'."

Dr Watson smirked at his friend's usage of an Americanism – his moustache, flecked with grey, curling upwards. I merely remained blank faced and rooted to the spot, like a naughty schoolboy whose headmaster hadn't quite finished disciplining him yet.

Chapter Seven

"Do not be too alarmed Mr Manders, this task is well within your scope. To employ another new-fangled phrase, this extra-curricular excursion will seem like a 'busman's holiday'. I already possess the location of the letter. The journalist has asked a friend of his, the manager of Hatchard's of Piccadilly, to store the letter in the shop's safe. And as to the combination Mycroft, has called in another favour and furnished us with that information also. The safe is located in the manager's office, behind a portrait of the store's original owner, John Hatchard. I would advise you and Mr Raffles to leave an accoutrement of his trade at the scene and take any money from the safe to disguise the true nature of the break-in. You will of course, pass on any money stolen from the safe – and Dr Watson here will shortly make a large purchase of books from the shop to endow a public library. Please also advise Mr Raffles that should you be apprehended, the blame for the crime must rest on you both squarely. I will deny knowledge of any involvement – and the word of Sherlock Holmes will bowl out for a duck that of Mr A.J. Raffles. Watson, would you kindly give the combination to Mr Manders?"

Dr Watson here handed me a slip of paper containing a set of six digits.

"Now, finally, I wish to convey to Mr Raffles that I am not ordering you to carry out this task. I am no blackmailer Mr Manders. I am merely asking Mr Raffles to do a good turn for someone who has, by keeping your names out of the newspapers and assizes, done you a good turn. I am asking him a favour, as if I were his brother-in-law – even one who he may dislike for having had an affair. Now, unless you have any questions Mr Manders, our business is concluded."

I stood still in shock and, I think, nodded. I felt lightheaded, like a man who had just been told the date of his execution. I cursed Raffles' absence, as he was my compass and I was all at sea without him. The detective looked at me a little strangely, or scornfully, that I should still be standing there after I had been dismissed – but Dr Watson kindly took me by the arm and led me out. I clasped the top of the banister to steady myself and, before heading down the stairs, caught the following exchange behind the closed sitting room door.

"Do you think that we can trust these fellows with Mycroft's mission?"

"I have every faith in Mr Raffles, Watson, albeit less so his nervous counterpart. Did I ever tell you that I once saw Raffles play at Lord's? He had an arm ball that not even I could rightly detect. But enough of cricket, musketeers and political scandals. We have far more grave concerns. The Napoleon of crime must meet his Waterloo."

Chapter Eight

Raffles returned from Truro the following day. Although I left a message with the doorman of the Albany to ask him to come and see me as soon as possible, with the matter being of the utmost importance, my friend still duly visited his tailor on Conduit Street first and then dropped off his bats into Lilywhite's to be oiled.

My eyes were ringed with sleeplessness and I flustered upon greeting Raffles. I was a heady cocktail of relief and anxiety upon seeing my dear companion's face. Yet despite my hysterical manner (I perhaps appeared more desperate in my behaviour than I was even upon the Ides of March), Raffles remained imperiously calm - which in some way heightened my frantic state, believing that he hadn't entirely comprehended the direness of the situation.

"Bunny, sit down and take two deep breaths before you utter another word. All will be well," he finally stated, in both an authoritative and fraternal tone. He proceeded to pour us a large whisky each. He then sat down himself, holding a finger up in the air to convey that I should still desist from speaking (or rather babbling).

"This seems like a two Sullivans predicament," he remarked, whilst extracting two of his cigarettes from his elegant, engraved silver cigarette case (a gift from his friend and fellow cricketing genius Kumar Shri Ranjitsinhji, or 'Ranji' as everybody called him). "Now, dear Bunny, just begin at the beginning and speak with the economy and clarity of your journalism."

And so I recounted the events of the previous twenty-four hours or so. Raffles interrupted me a couple of times upon points of detail but for the most part he just sat there, receptive and composed. The look on his face was akin to that he wore when playing baccarat, where one had more chance of reading ancient Persian than reading Raffles' reaction to the cards he had been dealt. His sapphire-blue eyes could be the soul of enthusiasm (for cricket, crime, women, poetry) or equally they could prove the soul of insouciance (for all of the aforementioned things also).

A pregnant pause ensued after I finished my report – but then my partner in crime finally responded after talking another sip of whisky and blowing a spiral of smoke up into the heavens, either wishing to choke the angels perhaps or have them partake in earthly pleasures too.

"That's good cricket, to request rather than order us to carry out the job," Raffles emitted, shaking his head and smiling as he did so. The gesture resembled that of when Raffles would be bowled by a jaffa. Although slightly melancholy not to get a score, he still couldn't help but admire the ball and wistfully grinned accordingly.

"I had hoped that I would stay off Mr Holmes' telegraph. This is a fine malt by the way Bunny. I regret not being here so as to have accompanied you to Baker Street. Our protector – or prosecutor, depending on which way you look at it – seems a queer fellow. But there is no doubting his brilliant mind. As much as I would have liked to cross wits, as oppose to swords, with him I probably would have, akin to your good self, remained shocked and reverent in his presence. We shall of course assent to his request, partly out of gratitude for not snitching on us these past months. And, as much as I enjoy taking the odd risk and consider myself not without some pluck, I do not wish to make an enemy of Sherlock Holmes. I'm well aware that I play down the order to him in the batting line-up of life.

I downed the rest of my whisky, reckoning that I should start storing up the Dutch courage as early as possible.

Chapter Nine

"We shall carry out the job tomorrow night. Pass me the slip of paper with the combination on it."

And in three seconds Raffles committed to memory that which took me thirty seconds to take in. "If you pack our second choice stethoscope so we can leave it at the scene. Even with our first choice and swathes of luck we probably couldn't crack the safe that way, but the police won't know that. I know we are just dealing with a bookshop, but pack our other tools also. Hope for the best, plan for the worst. I never imagined that I would ever be planning to turn over a bookshop though – and Hatchard's at that. I am very fond of the store and its staff. At least we will have the place to ourselves Bunny. It'll be a blessing not to bump into the likes of Wilde or Bernard Shaw, accidentally popping in to check the sales of their books or have some fawning American tourist recognise them. Did I tell you I once encountered Ann Radcliffe there? She is able to put a sentence together much better than an outfit. She was wearing a dress that lacked style even when it was in fashion. And we would have needed to use the crowbar you are about to pack to remove her caked on make-up. She asked me if I would like her to base a character in one of her novels on me. I was about to reply that I feared I wasn't one dimensional enough for her work but Wilde came over and rescued me from an awkward moment. It was the first time that I'd ever been grateful for his company. I left them to discuss fashion tips with one another whilst I made my purchases. I bought works by Conrad and Chesterton if I remember correctly. The first, the critics have not been kind enough to – and in regards to the latter they have perhaps been too kind. But I warrant that I am now being as garrulous and as self-centred as an author, Bunny. Tell me more of what you have been up to."

Aside from the events of the past day or so, which I had already relayed, my days since Raffles' departure had been pretty colourless. I had written an article, which would soon be used to stoke someone's kindling. Although I had played some cards and visited Boodles I must confess to you, which I couldn't to my companion, that I had spent most of my time wondering what Raffles had been up to. In regards to Boodles, fellow club members would often come up to me and ask after Raffles – and if I would be meeting him that evening. Upon hearing that he was away, friends would, in various degrees of subtlety, slope off to talk to someone else. I did not blame them. Even I found myself uninteresting – and uninterested – when out of Raffles' orbit. Holmes had called me his Boswell, but yet I also considered myself Sancho Panza to Raffles' Don Quixote. I soon found myself inquiring about my friend's time in Truro. Had he found his Dulcinea del Toboso? Also, I asked him about the cricket.

"My figures were satisfactory. Thankfully the figures of our host's daughter – and her cousin Lucy – were more than satisfactory however," he replied whilst smiling into his whisky tumbler and stubbing out another Sullivan.

Chapter Ten

Being in the half-light, surrounded by books, reminded me of being back at school again. Part of my duties fagging for Raffles all those years ago, was to fetch books from the library for him after hours. One term he would read the Augustan canon (devouring Horace, Virgil and Ovid), the next term he would apply himself to philosophy (Hume, Locke, Mill). Yet A.J. Raffles would still devoutly consider himself to be a 'lazy' student.

The thick crimson carpet was spongy beneath our feet as we climbed the stairs. Portraits of hoary, disapproving men glared at us from the walls. Finding the pictures and deathly quiet eerie, I turned to my friend and tried to strike up a conversation.

"I wonder which politician is the prospective victim of the letter's contents."

"I doubt that I'll have much sympathy for him, whoever he is. So many of them behave like bastards, whether it be towards their wives or the electorate. Lies trip off their tongues like leg glances off Ranji's bat. There's less fiction in Dumas than there is in their manifestos. A plague on all their houses."

"We are on the third floor, where the shelves of cricket books are," I replied, changing the subject – implying that Raffles might wish to pick out the odd book as a perk of the job.

"I love playing the game dearly old chap, but when not occupying the crease, or bowling at the other end, I try not to think about it. He who knows only of cricket knows nothing of cricket, a sage man once said."

We continued to climb the stairs and reached the top floor offices to the shop. Raffles warmed up his hands, now a little numb from the cold, and removed his skeleton key to open the door to the manager's office. He made easy work of the lock, as if it were the equivalent of someone bowling him a dolly of a full-toss and Raffles cover driving for four. Perhaps we would indeed make it back to the Albany before the ice in my drink melted, I thought to myself. But, as I once overheard Disraeli say at a party, 'Man plans, God laughs.'

Chapter Eleven

The office was relatively small and non-descript, neither religiously tidy nor a mess, neither opulent nor Spartan. I made sure to close the curtains so that not even the slightest crack of light could escape. A large desk, littered in a semi-orderly fashion with invoices and correspondence, dominated the room. A small fireplace sat opposite to the desk.

"It looks like we may well have to pour you another gin and tonic when we get back Bunny," Raffles exclaimed with a wistful sigh.

He had carefully lifted the accomplished portrait of John Hatchard off the wall, but he was confronted by a locked oak door between him and the safe. Experience – or perhaps the writings of Virgil and Horace – had taught Raffles to remain stoical in the face of such setbacks however.

"It's best you light a small fire to keep us warm while we work. The fog will conceal any plumes of smoke."

I duly lit a small fire, taking pleasure in burning a rival newspaper to that which I wrote for whilst doing so. It soon murmured and then crackled in the background.

We could not pick the lock, nor jemmy the door open. The scene was akin to that of when we broke into the Bond Street jewellers. I stood next to Raffles with a lantern in one hand and rock oil in the other (employed to reduce the noise). This time however, Raffles kept his jacket on as he cut out the lock by drilling a number of holes around it with a brace and bit. Again the holes numbered thirty two in total, albeit where as in Bond Street the task had taken forty seven minutes, Raffles took just forty two to best this door. It was always mesmerising to watch him at work. His being was infused with as much dedication and skill cutting around a lock as when he would carve out a half century at Lord's or the Kennington Oval.

"Thank you Bunny," he remarked once the door was open. He had little to thank me for, but I was always grateful to be of any assistance. "Now let's see if Mycroft's intelligence is as penetrating as his brother's," Raffles added, smirking at his own pun. "By heavens it is!" he exclaimed with a chuckle as the tumblers clicked into place and the thick steel door squeaked open.

I blew air out of my cheeks in relief. We would soon be back at the Albany. All would indeed be well, as Raffles had promised.

"It doesn't look like there's much money in books," he said whilst extracting a meagre number of notes from the safe. Raffles then quickly sifted through the various papers. He soon found our letter, yellow with age amidst the new white correspondence. Without studying the missive too much he carefully placed it in the side pocket of his jacket. In order not to arouse the suspicion that the safe had been broken into for the letter alone Raffles also removed a number of other documents (ones which he decided would not inconvenience the store too much if stolen) and gave them to me to stuff into our carpet bag.

The sound of rustling papers was dramatically succeeded however by the unmistakable click behind me of a revolver being cocked. I froze, whilst the eel returned and frantically slithered up and down my spine again. The singular Raffles however merely rolled his eyes, annoyed rather than petrified.

Chapter Twelve

"I am glad that I gave into the temptation to check upon my investment this evening."

The pistol he held was small, but lethal nevertheless. The journalist had an adenoidal voice. Squinting, beady eyes sat over an aquiline nose. An ill-fitting funeral black suit was worn upon a spindly frame. He was not the first journalist I had ever encountered to own both a supercilious and stoat-like air. I just hoped that he would not be the last.

"Put your hands up where I can see them."

I obliged more quickly than Raffles. I must have appeared as pale as the ghost that I was in danger of turning in to.

"Who are you working for? Where is it?" the journalist demanded, rather than asked. His slicked-back, oiled hair was the same shade as the barrel of his gun.

"I don't work for no one but me guv'nor. The score's not been great, but seeing as you're carrying that you can 'ave whatever you want from the box. What is this lark anyway?"

Doubt and confusion crept into the journalist's haughty expression upon hearing the Cockney accent. As well as his voice Raffles also mercurially altered his entire posture and manner. I always maintain that the crease's gain was the stage's loss, such was A.J. Raffles' ability to inhabit a role.

"I just want a certain old letter from the safe that you have just cracked. Or my next commission may be to write your obituaries, whether you're working for that conniving peer or some East End thug."

"Old letter? Oh, do you mean this fella?" Raffles replied. He then reached into his jacket pocket and in one swift, but graceful movement, screwed up the paper into a ball and bowled it across the room – and into the fireplace in a perfect arc. If the journalist had been a sports reporter he would have perhaps recognised the smooth and distinctive action, even in the half-light.

Our foe's eyes widened in shock and terror as though someone had just thrown a thousand pound cheque, with the journalist's name upon it, into the flames. He raced to the fireplace to rescue his asset, but before he could do so I ran and rugby tackled him to the ground. He landed with a judder upon the carpet, his attention still fixed upon the ball of paper crimpling and blackening in the fire. The gun spilled from his hand. You may judge that self-preservation had caused me to act so courageously – but more so I was worried that the journalist may have turned his gun upon my friend, in a fit of anger and retribution.

Raffles and I didn't need to tell each other to then bolt out of the door. I pulled on the handle as Raffles quickly used his skeleton key to lock the door and shut the nefarious hack in the office.

"Good work Bunny," he whispered whilst warmly clasping my shoulder, after the door was secure. "You are worth a thousand John Littles or Alan-a-Dales."

My soul soared upon hearing those words, both at the time of hearing them and now as I recall them.

We ran down the stairs, a mere blur in the eyes of the various portraits hanging upon the walls. Our feet pounded upon the carpet to the same rhythm of the journalist thumping upon the locked office door with his fists. Again, Raffles courteously held the backdoor open for me as we slipped out into Jermyn Street and disappeared into the fog and darkness.

Chapter Thirteen

"Not even Dr Watson himself, when playing for Blackheath Rugby Club, could have tackled that man the way you did this evening old chap," Raffles cheerfully exclaimed as he handed me a freshly poured gin and tonic back at the Albany.

"And not even Dr Grace could have defended the delivery you bowled into the fireplace," I replied – and then clinked glasses with my friend.

All was well. Even the fog outside was dissipating, revealing a bulbous moon and glittering night sky. The fog of cigar smoke infused our elegant but homely chamber however. The clock upon the chimney-piece struck three. I asked Raffles if he would like to accompany me to 221b Baker Street in the morning to tell Sherlock Holmes about the evening's events.

"I am of course tempted, but I would rather keep my distance. It may turn out that Holmes could dislike me – and it'll be Inspector Lestrade, rather than some odious hack, that interrupts us during our next job. Or, perhaps even worse, Holmes may take to me and be compelled to employ us for some future fool's errand. And by Jove that will never do! We're too old to be Baker Street Irregulars. No, Mr Holmes and I may well meet each other one day – but it will not be in this chapter of my life if I can help it."

"Aye and doing a supposed service to your country isn't the most lucrative of trades," I remarked. "You haven't made any money this week I fear."

Raffles shook his head to dismiss my concern however and asserted,

"Money lost – little lost. Honour lost – much lost. Pluck lost – all lost. Tonight has revealed how you still retain your honour and pluck Bunny. In another life you could have even been a musketeer. One for all, and all for one."

We proceeded to hold our tumblers aloft and then chimed them together, in the absence of any swords.

Chapter Fourteen

The following day, when I was just about to send a note to Baker Street to arrange a meeting and report upon our success, the sandy-haired Baker Street Irregular descended upon me again like some slightly less than divine Hermes, and informed me that Mr Sherlock Holmes was free to see me at four o'clock that afternoon.

Mrs Hudson, smelling of a mixture of lavender and freshly baked scones, again showed me up to the sitting room. Holmes was again in a dressing gown, albeit of a different design. His hair was unkempt and sprouted outwards in a bird's nest of tangents, as though he had spent the evening tossing and turning in his sleep or scratching his head when awake. His aspect was a little glassy, as though he was being fuelled by a stimulant. He was again sat in his large chair. All manner of newspapers, maps and missives were splayed upon his lap and the arms of the chair, as well as on the table next to him and the floor. His fingertips were stained with so much ink as to make any printer feel deficient.

Thankfully Dr Watson was also in attendance, nestling in an armchair close to Holmes', smoking his pipe contentedly and readying himself with a notepad and pen should Holmes wish his companion to record anything.

The clock upon the mantle chimed four.

"Thank you for your punctuality again Mr Manders. It is an under-appreciated virtue nowadays. You may begin your report. Leave nothing out, although please do not prattle on like the more florid members of your tribe." Holmes did not even look up when addressing me, scrivener-focused as he was upon scanning the sea of papers around him. Reading, filing (it seems there was a system) or discarding the material. Occasionally he would interrupt me with the odd question, such as asking me how large the letter was and which pocket did Raffles store the letter in and how close I came into contact with the document. Upon doing so he would survey my countenance intently, his inquisitive glare burrowing into my eyes – and into my soul. I ended my report by handing the money we took from the safe over to Dr Watson (Raffles had made sure to grab the carpet bag upon exiting the office, whilst still leaving the second choice stethoscope behind).

"Your account tallies with my enquiries. It seems that you have saved the venerated statesman and his recent lineage from ill repute, although I dare say that he will generate a scandal from his own volition sooner rather than later. Without the letter however the journalist will not be able to corroborate his accusations and should any newspaper publish, they will be damned. I feel little sympathy for the journalist in question. Although I am for the freedom of the press, your brethren are not beyond reproach Mr Manders and they often trumpet the public interest when the sounds of rapaciousness and tittle-tattle can clearly be heard in the background."

I nodded in agreement at his well-made point, although I dare say I would have nodded in agreement with the fearsome Sherlock Holmes even if I disagreed with him.

"Please pass on my thanks to Mr Raffles. My faith in him was well placed. He is indeed a gentleman and a thief. It seems I may have underestimated you however Mr Manders. You were uncommonly courageous and quick-witted in a crisis – and Mr Raffles is fortunate to have you as a friend and accomplice. I may not always thank Watson for putting me in the public eye through his colourful stories – but by God I owe him my life and reputation for a number of episodes which remain outside of the public domain. Without him I would be nothing."

Dr Watson here shook his head and coughed a little upon his own pipe smoke.

"Don't listen to him Mr Manders. When Holmes is not making me red-faced through my exasperation at some of his more peculiar traits, he makes me blush through unwarranted flattery. Enough now Holmes," Dr Watson gently chided.

I imagined that this was perhaps the closest that the old married couple would ever come to a heated argument.

"I shall not commend you to my brother however. It may spark the idea that he could commission you and Mr Raffles for some future enterprise. How like Mycroft it would be to regularly employ a cracksman to keep, rather than to extract, his skeletons in the closet. Please also pass on to Mr Raffles that I only have a desire to see his name in the papers next to some excellent bowling figures. Although some of his neighbours are doubtless the greatest swindlers in the land, the Albany is still preferable to Newgate."

I again nodded my head.

"Now finally Mr Manders, I wish you to make a promise to me. If ever you or Mr Raffles are summoned to a meeting with a Professor James Moriarty, in lieu of your services, you must vow to make straight for Baker Street before you make your appointment. I have forgiven you and Mr Raffles for past indiscretions, but I will show no mercy should you defy me in this matter. Do you understand?"

I nodded my head more vociferously than ever as Holmes' glare now almost seared a mark upon my soul, so that I would not forget my promise. There was a storm worn upon his brow as he mentioned this Professor Moriarty that made my heart quake. As Raffles could dramatically alter his manner in a second, from brooding to cheerfulness, so too did Holmes here smile and cordially utter –

"Now I believe that concludes our business. That will be all

Mr Manders. I have urgent work to attend to. In regards to that big fish I made reference to frying at our last meeting, we are about to turn up the heat," the detective expressed with relish. "Watson, would you please show Mr Manders out?"

Dr Watson rolled his eyes at the mild inconvenience of getting up and showing me to the door, which was but a few steps away, but he obliged his friend.

"Goodbye Mr Manders."

"Goodbye Dr Watson."

We shook hands and I departed. Mrs Hudson kindly made me a gift of half a dozen scones and some clotted cream as she bid me a good day when I reached the foot of the stairs and she showed me out.

Chapter Fifteen

That same evening I arranged to have dinner with Raffles, partly so I could relay to him the responses of the famous detective to the events at Hatchard's. We were also due to meet C.B. Fry at the Savile Club (of which I had recently become a member) at eleven o'clock. Raffles and I had agreed upon supper in Boodles before that however – and we would first rendezvous at the Albany for a few drinks. Once we were in the company of Fry it would be difficult, for either of us, to get a word in edgeways if he was in a mood to hold court. Yet we both loved 'Charles III' dearly (our nickname for Fry, derived from an article in *Vanity Fair* which titled him thus after recounting all his accomplishments/records as a cricketer, footballer and athlete – whilst still only twenty-one!).

Raffles opened the door with a gin and tonic in one hand - which he passed to me - and a letter in the other. *The* letter!

"By God is that Aramis' letter?!" I ejaculated, nearly spilling my drink as I did so.

"Yes," Raffles responded, as calm as you like – his eyes twinkling as much as any star in the cosmos.

"But how?" I spluttered, this time spilling a little of my drink.

"You see, but do not observe," he wittily replied, quoting a saying of Sherlock Holmes'. "What you saw last night was me tossing into the fire a love letter from Lucy Rosebery, cousin to the daughter of my host over the weekend, rather that of Rene D'Aramis, the musketeer and spy."

"You are a card Raffles, a knave!" I shook my head in slight disbelief and grinned. "You are also as secretive as a spy. Why did you not tell me that you were still in possession of the letter last night?" I tried to be mad at my friend for keeping me in the dark yet again, but I couldn't.

"Elementary, my dear Bunny. Holmes' hawk-like nose would have smelled a rat should you have tried to lie to him about the letter going up in flames. You are too honest for your own good sometimes, but I would not want you any other way my friend."

"What will you do now with the document?"

"Nothing. Like Holmes, I'm no blackmailer. I will keep the letter to use as a bargaining chip should we ever get pinched. I'll place it in a safety deposit box tomorrow. As long as we never have to darken a courtroom, the letter will never see the light of day," he issued, placing the paper upon his desk for him to attend to in the morning.

I here asked Raffles if it was wise to try and out-fox Holmes, but that incorrigible twinkle which lit up Jermyn Street returned to his expression and he gamely exclaimed,

"A man's reach must exceed his grasp, dear boy, or what the dickens is a heaven for?"

Over a couple of drinks I went through my meeting with Holmes and Dr Watson. Upon finishing Raffles savoured the taste of his Sullivan, drained his whisky and announced,

"Now, let us draw a line under the events of the past few days, close the chapter. It seems that we are, blessedly, small fry for Holmes. Make Mrs Hudson's scones last Bunny, for God willing you will not have cause to visit 221b Baker Street for some time. We will keep our promise though, if ever this Professor Moriarty gets in touch." Raffles glanced at his pocket watch and added, "But let us now visit Boodles, before they run out of the duck terrine or John Dory."

Chapter Sixteen

Most of the remainder of our evening passed without incident, aside from some gangly drunk bumping into Raffles outside the Albany and our waiter at the club spilling half a glass of Pol Roger over my new trousers. It was a night for clumsiness, in more ways than one.

Unfortunately, Raffles' fears were realised in that the club had but one serving of the duck terrine left by the time we arrived – which he insisted that I have. The John Dory had completely finished however, but we could compliment the sommelier upon his choice of claret to go with our lamb. If only I could compliment our waiter on his steady hand. As was the case in most instances when Raffles dined at the club, he was approached by either friends or fans complimenting him on his cricket season, or inviting him to play at their houses the following season. Raffles always gave a cordial, but non-committal reply.

In between courses I asked my friend about Lucy Rosebery. I was normally chary in inquiring about Raffles' affairs, as I envisioned that one day he would inform me that he had found his intended, and our life of crime – and gentlemanly conviviality – would be over. But I was curious about this young woman who had written a love letter to Raffles so soon after they had first met.

"Although I ventured to Truro to, in part, court her cousin Margaret I found myself spending an increasing amount of time in Lucy's company – and missing not Margaret as I did so. She is uncommonly pretty Bunny, with a slim figure hewn from vigorous exercise rather than under eating. Her long blonde tresses seem spun from gold and her blue eyes, unlike how mine can sometimes be, are never cold. She has something about her my friend, a quality. Or should I say qualities? Aye, she has honour, pluck – and money," he enthused. Such was the mischievous gleam in his aspect that I discerned not how much weight he attached to this last asset. Even after all these years there were times when I could still only read Raffles about as well as I could pick his off break.

"Unfortunately she has recently joined the suffragettes, but nobody's perfect. But for all of her spirited and modish opinions about emancipation and the lower classes she still possesses an old-fashioned grace and charm. Put simply, she doesn't bore me Bunny. I am inclined to see her again, when she comes down to London next month. I'm unsure as to whether she's intending to save womankind or the lower classes during her week here, but hopefully she will also make time to save this scoundrel. But do not worry, the champagne is not going to my head – far more was spilled over your new trousers. I have not lost my heart to Ms Rosebery. I am still much more likely to wear the ball and chain of Newgate, to that of matrimony. But what of you old chap – any news?"

My news and conversation always seemed too pale in comparison with Raffles', but I mentioned how the Strand Magazine had asked me to write a piece on London's bookshops. Are they leaders or followers of taste?

"Fry has also just been sounded out on whether he wants to write some articles on football and cricket for them. He wants my advice, having written for the Strand before. I will tell him to go ahead. The magazine is not just full of the kind of potboilers that Mr Holmes derides so much."

I was here interrupted by a waiter, who brought over to the table two of the club's famous Orange Fools.

"But what of your next job?" I remarked in a hushed tone, unable to suppress my sense of intrigue and excitement however.

"The game is afoot on that score my friend – and again the job will be close to home. Indeed it couldn't be closer. But let me leave it there for now."

Shortly afterwards the clock struck ten. We ordered two small ports whilst asking for the bill.

"As much as he won't be short of company, or rather an audience, we should head over to the Savile to meet Fry soon. I can picture him now, showing members the perfect cover drive using an umbrella as a bat and an apple for a ball." Raffles joked.

"I agree. We would not want to miss the final act to our evening."

The waiter brought over our ports and the bill. I went to sign the chit but Raffles held up his hand.

"Please, it's on me old chap. I insist. You can get the drinks at the Savile."

Raffles reached into his inside pocket for a pen. He rummaged around in slight befuddlement. I was about to ask if he had mislaid his wallet when he placed the item upon the table. A pen top materialised. Yet still he continued to search for something on his person. He checked all of his pockets twice, thoroughly. It was rare for that smooth, handsome brow to be creased in concern. His blue eyes even lost their lustre, as if put out by a blunt instrument. He then just paused and pensively shut his eyes, as if replaying a memory.

"What's wrong my friend?" I asked, perturbed in sympathy.

"I have a horrible suspicion that the final act of this evening could now prove tragic," Raffles remarked cryptically, as much to himself as to me. He quickly signed off on the bill, leaving a far too generous tip for our dunderhead waiter.

"Come Bunny, we must make straight for the Albany."

Chapter Seventeen

The rain first coughed down upon us when leaving the club in St James', but by the time we reached Piccadilly the heavens opened. I nigh on had to run to keep pace with my friend, who strode on like a man possessed, his overcoat billowing in the snarling wind. When retrieving our coats from the cloakroom of the club I had questioned Raffles again on the dramatic change in his behaviour.

"I do not wish to yet say anything Bunny, for fear of appearing paranoid or fantastical. But by God, this is the night that either makes me, or forgoes me quite. Reynard may have well been out-foxed."

The rain chilled my already bloodless pate as we dodged around hansom cabs and weaved through the sodden throng occupying the pavement. I began to wish that I was in possession of my revolver, such were my foreboding thoughts. I warrant that there had been times when Raffles had run between the wickets with less urgency, compared to how he marched on now down Piccadilly. He began to mutter to himself,

"When you have eliminated the impossible, whatever remains, *however* improbable, must be the truth... But not even I would have taken such a risk."

We were greeted at the entrance to the Albany by the ever-amiable doorman Clarence, who made some comment about the weather. Yet – and this is the only instance I can remember of my friend ever being discourteous to the staff of the building – Raffles ignored the man and bounded up the stairs, three steps at a time.

I was panting heavily – and Raffles looked as if he were about to snort fire – as he opened the door to his apartment and rushed to his desk.

"The devil! The rogue!" Raffles exclaimed, striking the antique walnut bureau (which had once been the property of Coleridge). Mystification and concern vied for sovereignty in my being.

"The fiend! The genius!"

As I tentatively approached my friend his anger began to mercurially transform into amusement – and admiration. Rather than pound his beloved bureau, he now slapped his desk in celebration, or congratulations. The congenial twinkle returned to his aspect, like the sun coming out from behind the clouds.

"The gambler! The poet!" he trumpeted, before filling the air with sweet laughter. I couldn't help but grin in sympathy, albeit my relief was still allied to being mystified.

"We have been humbugged Bunny, by the Napoleon of Justice! Our loss of the letter – and the immunity from prosecution it may have provided – is offset by the fact that we may well be immortalised one day by Dr Watson. The drunk, who nigh on knocked me over outside the Albany this evening, was none other than Holmes! He pick-pocketed me, relieving me of my skeleton key – which he then used to break into my apartment. The man is a marvel. Perhaps I should have heeded your advice and placed mousetraps in my pockets."

Again he laughed, clapping me on the shoulder.

"Look, there upon the desk Bunny. I dare say that I will treasure his note more than any written by our monsieur Aramis."

Moving aside the skeleton key which lay upon it, I picked up the note. Perhaps it was the cold, but my hands trembled a little in excitement - or trepidation.

'*It takes a thief to catch a thief. S.H.*'

I smiled.

"It's Everybody's Fight"

Pat Hobby shook his head in sadness at the news on the radio. The world was at war. His next whisky would be a double. France had fallen. Great Britain was standing alone. Hitler and his Nazi thugs controlled Europe. Pat spared a thought for Jakob Lowenstein, a scriptwriter friend who had married a French woman and moved to Paris ten years ago. Pat and Jakob had shared many a drink and secretary together back in the good old days. They had worked on a number of pictures together too. Lowenstein had been good with dialogue, Hobby good on structure. For the first time in a long time Pat offered up a prayer, to the great barman in the sky, that Jakob would be okay, or that he would get out of France in time.

Suddenly a prayer was answered – which granted had been offered up some time ago – in that Vince Malley, the barman and owner of Malley's Tavern, poured Pat a free drink. The half-Irish, half-Italian, but wholly American Malley poured himself a large whisky too.

"We need to get into the fight soon," Malley exclaimed, scrunching his face up in frustration or belligerence.

"It's not our fight to get into," replied another barfly, neither frustrated nor belligerent – though a little irked that he had not received a free shot as well.

"It's everybody's fight," Pat Hobby announced, as much to himself as to the bar, quoting a line from a First World War movie that Jakob Lowenstein had worked on, *The Doughboys*. Pat, more one to concern himself with the gossip on the lot and in Variety, also remembered the news reports about the night of broken glass in Germany a few years back. His face looked even more careworn than usual, his eyes even more red-rimmed.

"It's everybody's fight," the producer Ion Tinder proclaimed, chomping upon a large cigar with more enthusiasm than usual. "This war could be the shot in the arm that the movie business has been waiting for. War pictures sell, as sure as night follows day. Even surer in fact! This war could mean boom time again. But we can't stand still and hope that it starts raining money. Every director, producer, actor, best boy, screenwriter, publicist and usherette needs to grasp this opportunity with both hands. And I need you to grasp this opportunity I'm about to give you Pat."

Pat Hobby sat in the producer's office, half asleep. He would only stir once the subject of money was brought up. Money he was willing to grab with both hands. Opportunities were liable to slip through his fingers.

"It could lead to some good money and even a writing credit. The British actor Nigel Chester is in town. He was a star on the London stage and has recently conquered Broadway. He's just won an award for acting in some play called *The Berry Orchard*, penned by some Russian guy. That reminds me, I must get my secretary to get onto this guy's agent to ask if the author has sold the film rights. Anyway, this Nigel Chester could be the next big thing. He'd be perfect playing an RAF officer. He's got the clean looks and the right British accent for the movies. He's like Basil Rathbone but younger and with a moustache. His agent has indicated that he wants to get into film. I want you to take these scripts over to him – we're putting him up in a condo on the coast – and persuade him that Hollywood beats Broadway. If you convince him to sign up for one of the projects then I'll give you a credit and you can help out with the script. How does that sound?"

"How much?"

"Forty bucks for the day, which'll include expenses."

"I'll do it for fifty."

They settled on forty.

"That's more than any other delivery boy gets paid. And if you deliver Chester, then we can add a zero onto the next cheque."

The glowing red of dusk induced in Pat a craving for a Bloody Mary as he drove along the winding coastal road. He could taste the salt in the air from the foaming sea. Yet unfortunately the taste of salt would not be followed by lime and a shot of tequila. As consolation for the absence of a Bloody Mary and shot of tequila Pat took out his hip flask containing a fine enough malt whisky.

The condo was large and sat upon an isolated part of the coast. The studio often rented the property to stars or producers who needed to dry out or escape from their wives or mistresses. Chester answered the door himself. The theatre critic for the *New York Times* had described the actor as "elegant" and "quintessentially British." Hobby thought he looked thin and pale.

"Come in Mr Hobby, Mr Tinder phoned ahead. Thank you for travelling all this way. Let me help you with that," Chester remarked, as he unburdened Pat of the box containing the scripts. "Would you like a drink?"

Although the Brits stood alone, Pat Hobby would not allow one of them to drink alone.

Nigel Chester refilled his guest's glass – and his own – again. Who needs expenses? – Pat happily thought to himself. The forty-nine year old screenwriter was growing to like his host – and not just because of his finest single malt whisky. Chester was genuinely amiable and was fond of conversing, rather than just monologuing (unlike most actors, British or otherwise, Pat had encountered over the years). He was well dressed and well spoken, although as the evening wore on Chester relieved himself of his jacket and tie. His accent also started to slip – and the boy from south London commenced to creep out of the classically-trained thespian.

Hobby, after recounting something of his own background, learned that although the newspapers referred to Chester as being refined, part of the establishment and even aristocratic he was, in reality, the son of a milkman and a charwoman from Eltham. After starring in his first play in London, Chester had stepped out with both a Bowes-Lyon and a Rothschild. He began to make the society pages and continued to play the "English gent". And America loved the act more than anyone.

"I've come a long way you could say Pat. Too far. I'm now six thousand miles away from 'ome. My country's at war and the only uniform I'm looking to put on is one provided by a costume department. My mates in Eltham are signing up to enlist and I'm out 'ere looking to sign a film deal," the actor remarked with self-censure.

Shortly afterwards Chester excused himself and said he was heading off to bed, but yet he wasn't sleeping well and would try to look over a few of the scripts. He insisted that Pat stay the night however and showed him to a guest bedroom.

Shortly after the actor departed Hobby filled his hip flask up with his host's finest malt whisky and turned in too.

Sunlight glinted upon the churning ocean the following morning as Pat Hobby looked outside of his window. His stomach churned too, from his bout of drinking the previous night. Unused to the sea air - the fresh air - he had a headache. When Pat finally showered and dressed it was approaching midday. He found his host in the kitchen, a number of scripts splayed out upon the table before him, with a mug of coffee in his hand.

"Morning Pat. Hope you slept well. I've been looking over these scripts. There's one that shows promise and that I'd like to talk to Mr Tinder about. It still needs some work though –

and I was told you're good on structure. There's a scene I think that could use some work that I'd like you to take a look at. Of course if things come to fruition I'll arrange for you to come on board with the picture."

Pat Hobby first poured himself some coffee and then duly poured over the script. The scene concerned the protagonist's decision to give up his teaching position at Oxford, to enlist in the RAF. Chester asked the screenwriter to fill out the speech made by the hero, to make it more poignant or inspiring. Hobby replied that he would do his best, but that he asked to be able to work in private. The screenwriter took a pen, some paper, a mug of coffee and his hip flask out onto the condominium's balcony. Half an hour went by and the sheet of paper was still only marked by a squiggly line that Pat had made to check that the pen was working. He dozed off during the second half an hour he spent working out on the balcony. Yet soon after he woke up Hobby had an inspired idea. He would re-write a speech written by Jakob Lowenstein for the movie *The Doughboys*.

"There's no peace to be had with the Germans. There's no pact to be made with the Devil. It's fight, or be slain. Their enemy isn't just a country or even a nationality. The enemy for them is civil society as we know it. Their enemies are love and freedom... You say to me that it's not my fight, or that other men should take my place and stand in the line. No. You ask me whose fight this is? It's everybody's fight!"

"This is great Pat. You're great Pat," the actor announced upon reading over the scene. He then read over the words again and gulped, as if choking back tears or about to break down. He recovered however to remark, "I'm going to tell Tinder that I want to go ahead with the project – and I want you on board too."

No sooner did Chester finish that sentence than he was on the telephone to Ion Tinder to tell him the good news. He also sung

Pat's praises and spoke with a manic enthusiasm about wishing to proceed with the project immediately. When the actor finally passed the phone over to the screenwriter the producer mentioned how Hobby could expect him to add a zero to the cheque he was due to collect.

The warm, massaging rays of the afternoon sun and a few swigs of whisky from his hip flask brought the colour back into his cheeks as Pat Hobby drove back to Hollywood. He stopped off at Malley's Tavern – and bought Vince Malley a drink – on his triumphant return, before heading over to the studio to collect his cheque. He thought of what he might spend the money on. He would buy a new suit. He would also book a table at the Malabar or Sapphire Sea and finally pluck up the courage to ask out Alice Rowe, from the secretarial pool. He was back, he thought.

Pat was half-expecting to be given a cigar when he walked into Ion Tinder's office, in congratulations for delivering the actor. Instead the screenwriter received a face full of cigar smoke, as the producer spat out across his desk,

"You've been, quite literally, the author of your own demise this time Hobby."

"I, I don't understand," Pat replied, spluttering from the cigar smoke and confusion.

"I've just got off the phone from the bastard. He won't be signing up for any war picture, as he's decided to enlist and take part in the war for real. He'll be signing his own death sentence rather than any film deal now. Bastard actors!" Tinder shouted, chomping down so hard upon his cigar that it broke and nearly fell from his mouth. "And you're to blame. It seems you wrote something and he took it to heart so much that he wants to join the army. Chester said to tell you "it's everybody's fight" – that you'd understand. I bet you're regretting your dumb ass call to arms, no? - seeing as you won't now be getting a credit or that bonus."

Hobby tilted his head slightly and his eyes looked skyward, in reflection. He remembered again Jakob Lowenstein and the newspaper reports after Kristallnacht.

"No, I'm not," Pat replied.

*

Printed in Dunstable, United Kingdom